Kissmas Eve

USA TODAY BESTSELLING AUTHOR

SARA NEY & M.E. CARTER

KISSMAS EVE

CHAPTER 1

"If I ever get fired, I hope it's because of an office romance."
MEG

I love Christmas.

No. I mean—I love Christmas. Not just Christmas itself, but everything leading up to it. The crisp chill in the air and frost on the ground before the snow. Hustle and bustle and in town; I get stupid giddy when they finally hang the lights and the decorations on Main Street. It makes me feel nostalgic.

I love seeing a Santa on every corner. I love the sounds of the Salvation Army bells, always chip in spare change if I have it handy, and bundling up in the bright red coat I only get to wear from Thanksgiving, through December 30. It's an adorable, crimson pea coat and I added the greatest vintage rhinestone Santa pin to the lapel.

This year, strangely enough, I can't get into the Christmas spirit. I suppose it has to do with the fact that I just moved from Illinois to Dallas, Texas—and Dallas doesn't get cold for Christmas—it gets frigid at best. But according to Sheila, the woman whose cubicle is next to mine at work, 65 degrees is cold enough to cause *hypothermia*.

To me? Seeing lights and merriment *without* snow and *without* sub-zero temperatures just doesn't feel as festive. At least, not to this transplant.

And speaking of Sheila, I can hear her on the phone in her cubicle, tittering.

Which means she's on the phone with her boyfriend. Yes, the gray haired woman in the next cube over, twice my age and as jaded as they come, has a steady boyfriend.

And I don't.

"No you hang up…" I hear over the thin walls, cooing into the receiver of her office phone like a teenager. "No *you* hang up…." She giggles softly, sounding slightly dirty. For a brief moment, a sick part of me wonders what they'd been talking about. "I swear you make it so *hard* to keep my mind on my job, Neil."

I silently plead for him to do us both a favor and hang up.

I have work to do, but I can't get it done with this lovey-dovey going on the entire day.

It's very distracting. And frankly, kind of depressing.

Oh god, I'm jealous of Sheila.

I decide to text my best friend Tabitha; she's an author and loves hearing about shit like this. Not to mention, I miss her like crazy since I moved and not a day goes by that we don't message each other. Glancing at my clock, I notice it's almost noon, so she's probably taking a break to have lunch.

She does her writing at a quaint little coffee shop, even though her husband Collin built her the greatest home office; she says the chairs at home just aren't as comfortable, and the lattes aren't as hot Writers and their weird issues, I swear…

Meg: *I'm almost positive Sheila and Neil were just having phone sex.*

Tabitha: *Remind me again who Sheila is.*

Meg: *Her cubicle is next to mine at work, and I can hear everything that goes on.*

She just got off the phone with her boyfriend, and I swear they were, you know...

Tabitha: *You should ask to join them next time. Make it a threesome.*

Meg: *You're sick, do you know that?*

Tabitha: *I write romance novels; what kind of sympathy were you wanting from me?*

Meg: *You have KIDS! Two of them.*

Tabitha: *So? How do you think I got 'em? *wink wink**

Meg: *Good point.*

Tabitha: *What do you think the real problem is here?*

Meg: *What do you mean?*

Tabitha: *Do you really care that Sheila is having phone sex in her cubby, or are you just jealous you aren't having sex in yours. Oops, I mean PHONE sex. Hehe.*

Meg: *I would never have phone sex at work!!!!*

Tabitha: *Well, what about just regular sex?*

Meg: *Go back to work.*

Tabitha: *Thanks, I will. You just gave me a great idea to write about.*

Awesome. My best friend is going to *write* about sex, gets to *have* regular sex with her husband, and now I'm sitting at my desk at work, thinking about it. Sex, that is.

I stare at my computer monitor blankly, having lost total focus.

Don't get me wrong—I like my job.

In fact, I love it.

It's always been my ambition to become a sports agent; so landing a job at McGinnis Agency was a dream come true. I don't want to say I got lucky, but the candidates that I had to compete against to get this job were the top of their class at some of the best business schools around the country. Some say throwing your resume into the hiring ring at McGinnis is as competitive as an athlete entering the draft.

So many candidates, only a few spots on the McGinnis agent team.

Still unable to focus on work, even with a looming compensation contracts deadline approaching, I readjust the little plastic Rudolph on my desk, his little red nose shining and bright, just like the song. I'm about to check his batteries when a commotion at the front catches my attention, and I pivot in my chair as Jason Hart strolls past my cube.

Jason Hart.

NFL defensive lineman powerhouse.

Broadcasting personality.

Tall, broad shouldered, and larger than life, Mr. Hart is one of our most well-known football clients. A virtual hulk of a man, he towers above the gray particians of the cubicles that make up the seventh floor of our agency, and I tail his wake as he enters the office of the *one* person I haven't made an effort to talk to since I've been here.

Adam Roberts.

Agent and manager.

Marketing machine.

I sigh his name wistfully inside my head. Watch as he stands to greet his client, smoothing down the pleats of his dark gray slacks. The men shake hands, Adam slapping Mr. Hart on the back, then closing the door behind them both. Darn it, now I won't be able to hear his laugh.

It's subdued but strong, just like he is.

Fortunately, I can look my fill because Adam's office is made completely out of glass. It's like he's in a proverbial fish bowl, and I watch him like he's there just for my enjoyment. I can sneak glances and gaze at him all I want because he is right. There. All his dark, hot chocolaty brown hair and darker eyes, Adam is just as tall as Jason Hart. Just as formidable.

He steals my breath away.

Don't get me wrong; I don't just watch him because of his looks.

Adam Roberts is *brilliant*.

A managing member of the Talent Department, Adam's job is to direct and organize the professional—and media circus—that is the life of Mega Athlete Jason Hart. That includes supervising the public relations team when Jason's son was sick, and joining the Board of Directors of Mr. Hart's multi-million-dollar foundation, Hart to Heart.

He manages to make it seem effortless.

I sigh again, this time into my Elf coffee mug.

Obviously I'm drinking hot chocolate and not coffee, because there's no holiday spirit in *that*. I poke at a floating marshmallow, sipping it into my mouth with a soft slurp, trying to look busy while I covertly watch Adam invite Jason Hart to have a seat in one of his big, leather desk chairs.

I wonder distractedly if a brilliant, attractive bachelor like Adam would ever notice someone like me. Someone who can't resist her Santa leggings when the calendar strikes December 1. Someone who dons an ornament shaped purse and silver, dangly Christmas tree earrings.

Someone that doesn't exactly scream *Executive Management Girlfriend* material.

As I gaze through the glass of his office walls, my green eyes can't help wandering to the lavender necktie expertly knotted around his neck, and I wonder if he's the type to ever consider wearing one with tiny snowflakes on it. He's animated now, large hands gesturing as he speaks to his client, sleeves rolled to his elbows.

I find the whole picture incredibly *sexy*.

His forearms are incredible.

My eyes drift as he speaks, traveling over a full set of lips surrounded by the dark shadow of beard stubble.

Sexy.

His hair is still wet from an early morning shower, and I bet he smells as incredible as he looks—I've never let myself close enough to take a whiff. Another wistful sigh escapes my mouth, and when I prop my chin in my hands and lift my eyes—

Oh Scrooge.

Shoot. *Shit.*

Jason Hart is staring at me. *Staring.*

With a cocky smirk stretched across his handsome face.

Instantly my guilty eyes widen at being caught, cheeks flush before I jerk them away to look down at my monitor.

How embarrassing.

Then I have another horrifying thought: what if Jason Hart thinks I was staring at *him*? How unprofessional, ogling a *client*. And one that's married for heaven's sake! And famous. And so far out of my league it's laughable.

A scratchy, intrusive voice interrupts my woolgathering, and I give a start in my chair, almost dropping my mug. "Hey, Christmas Mary, what are you wearing to the office party tomorrow night?"

"Jesus Sheila, you scared the crap out of me! I thought you went back to work."

"Nope."

Of course she wouldn't be. Instead of tackling that mountain of paperwork I've noticed on her desk, it looks like she's spent the last ten minutes primping. Literally applying make-up as she speaks to me, circular pink compact, and crimson lipstick tube in her hands.

I swear, with as much lipstick as she puts on, it's a wonder Neil doesn't have permanently red stained lips. I tap my mug in thought—come to think of it, his lips always have been a little on the colorful side. Stained.

"What are you wearing to the office party tomorrow?" She repeats, blotting a pressed powder puff to her overly done face.

I squirm in my seat. "The party is right after work, right?"

"Six o'clock on the dot down in the lobby. Most people don't get there until closer to seven, but if you're not down there right away you miss out on the free booze. Band starts at eight."

"Don't most people just wear their work clothes?"

She shoots me a disapproving look. "Meg. This is the office *Christmas* party. This isn't an office Ugly Sweater Christmas party."

Wait. Did she just lower her eyes to my sweater when she said that?

"You can't wear your…" she stalls and waves her hand in a circle in my direction, like she's trying to find the words to describe what I'm wearing but can't quite find them. "Festivey… crazy…people of Walmart outfit. Look them up on the intranet system if you don't believe me."

I scoff. Like I would do that.

"Sheila, these leggings are so fun! And how did you know they were from Walmart! Four bucks—I couldn't just *leave* them there." I laugh. "Besides, they're festive and fun. This is the best time of year and the only time I can get away with dressing funky at work."

She crinkles her nose in disgust. "I didn't realize you actually got your clothes there. I thought it just looked that way. Now it all makes sense."

I try not to let her comments bother me. She can't ruin my holiday cheer. "Well, you've been here longer than I have. What do you think I should wear tomorrow? Will I be overdressed if I wear a fun sweater to the party?"

Sheila's eyes widen. "Overdressed? No. The ladies here get all decked out; dresses, sequins—the whole enchilada."

My brows shoot up, concerned. I nibble my lip. "They do?"

"Yes, but don't y'all worry; Deborah from accounting has a cosmetology degree. I'm sure she'd love to get her mitts on you."

"Deborah from accounting? Has a cosmetology degree *and* an accounting degree? Wow."

"And nails. She does a kick ass gel refill." Sheila takes a few seconds to study her manicure. "Her pedicures are shit, though, but don't you dare tell her I told you that."

I give my head a little nod, causing my silver tree earrings to jingle. "I won't."

Sheila waves a hand airily, and I notice her long, blood red nails. Yikes. "Let's finish this talk about your clothes, sugar. You can't wear…work clothes to the party."

"I can't?"

"Well. Some people can. Just not *you*. That outfit is hideous."

I look down at my beloved leggings. Sure, they aren't the *best* material money can buy—and yes, you can see right through them to my underwear when I bend over—but they're covered with Santa! If the women of the world can run around the entire year wearing those crazy, weird leggings everyone is buying on Facebook, then surely I can get away with some Santa heads all over *mine*.

"I'm wearing the most festive outfit in this entire office. See, my shirt has glitter on it," I argue.

"Yeah, I can see it."

"How is this not appropriate for the party?"

"Honey, for the women in this office, this is like the Super Bowl of man-hunting. They'll be showing up in four-inch heels and the most sophisticated outfits they can get their manicured claws on. You don't want to turn up lookin' like a bumpkin, do you?"

Fine. I'll be the first to admit I go a little overboard around the holidays, but during the rest of the year, I'm as professional as they come. Predictable and boring, if I'm being honest: navy pencil skirts down to my knees and white button down shirts. Heels. Sleek ponytails and pearls.

"Meg. Darlin. You forget the industry we work in." She says it gently, as if I'm not aware our company services some of the most physically fit, good-looking, men and women in the world. "I realize this will be your first Christmas party with us, but do you think it's just men from the *office* that will be there tomorrow? Clients come too, Meg. *Clients.*"

"Clients?"

"You know that quarterback who was just in Adam's office today?"

"He's not a quarterback."

"Whatever. The Holiday party is going to be packed with his teammates. Coaches. There will be hot, virile, athletic men galore. If you want the chance to nail one of them, you need to look the part."

"Wait. *Nail* one of them?"

Is she nuts? I would never dream of mixing business and pleasure—getting involved with a client? Plus, I think I read something in the Employee Handbook about fraternizing with clientele; it took me an entire week to read that thing.

"One of them might decide he actually likes you for you, but until then—you're going to have to change your clothes if you want to be the wife of Mr. Hot, *Hot* Bodied Sports Star," she says with a dreamy look on her face.

"I'm beginning to think you just work here for access to the athletes," I mutter. "Besides, don't you have a boyfriend?"

"Neil?" She laughs, a few loose strands of gray hair falling out of her top knot. "Oh honey, no. We're just having some fun."

Just having fun? This is news to me.

Trust me, I've seen the bouquets he's sent her—big, obscenely expensive ones—and have to hear about the places he takes her on weekends. Romantic restaurants, concerts, plays, and one time, a cabin by the lake.

"Are you sure *he* knows you're just having fun? Are you sure he's not…" Let see, how do I put this. "More *invested* in this than you think he is?"

She waves a hand, dismissively, charm bracelet jingling. "He's a nice distraction, Meg, but he knows he's temporary until the right man comes sailing through *those*," she stabs her index finger toward the embankment. "Those elevator doors over there."

I just shake my head. I should have known she didn't have any real interest in this job.

She barely does anything but gossip and flit around, and I'm a little disappointed in myself for not figuring it out sooner. I just assumed she likes short skirts for the breezy aspect.

"So. Back to the holiday party," she says clapping her hands together. "You need a new outfit."

I glance down at my red, tinsel covered sweater, then up toward Adam's office. "I don't *need* a new outfit."

"Sweetie, I'm afraid you do. We're going shopping."

"We are not going shopping." I can go on my own.

"Why not?" she asks, looking crestfallen.

"Because you don't actually *like* me."

To her credit, she tries really hard to not agree with me at first. Until she gives up the charade.

"Ok fine. I don't. But whether or not I like you is irrelevant because I like *shopping*."

"Well, I don't."

"Unless you're at Walmart," she mutters.

"Hey!"

"Really? You're going to deny it? You're wearing four dollar pants."

I shrug in acknowledgement, picking at the fabric hugging my thighs. Picking at Santa's little rosy cheeks. "But they're so cute."

"Honey, no. They're really not. It looks like you sat on Santa's face and it got stuck to your ass."

My mouth gapes. "Then you're looking too closely at my ass because, I'm wearing a sweater over it."

"You mean the sweater that hikes up the back every time you bend over to pick something up?"

I look down at the thick, warm, but *thin* material on my lap. Sure enough, it's stretched just enough that I can see straight through to Kris Kringle. He's staring up at me. "Well shit. Why didn't you tell me before now?"

"Because I have a running bet with Deborah about how long it will take you to figure it out. Don't tell her you know yet. If you hold out another week, I make twenty bucks. Fifty if you wear them again on Monday."

"Seriously? I'm the butt of office jokes now?"

"Only since that first week in December when it become obvious this was going to be a December thing. Before that we didn't really talk about you at all." She pauses, not giving me time to feel sorry for myself. "So let me take you shopping. *Please?* I promise to behave."

She begs as if she hasn't spent the last few minutes insulting me. "We'll get you something sparkly that hugs your curves. We'll—we'll even do a see through test on your ass so you don't flash anymore pink thong! Just don't tell Deborah."

I stand up and grab my favorite elf-hat shaped coffee mug, heading toward the break room. There isn't enough peppermint hot chocolate to get me through this day. Maybe I should consider dumping in whatever Sheila dumps into her coffee. "Thank you, Sheila, but I actually think I have the perfect outfit in my closet at home."

"You do?"

No, but she doesn't need to know that.

"Doesn't every woman?" I call over my shoulder, and catch the smile of approval on her face. She nods enthusiastically.

"Bring it tomorrow and meet us in the bathroom on the 4th floor. 5:30 sharp. I'll let Deborah know she can work her magic then. I can't wait for us to turn you into a real woman!"

I roll my eyes as I strut toward the break room, a secret smile playing on my lips.

Because if there's one thing I love besides Christmas, it's the *mall* at Christmas.

* * *

ADAM

I CAN BARELY CONCENTRATE on whatever Jason is saying as I watch the exchange between Meg and that old battle axe Sheila, then watch in earnest when Meg storms off toward the break room, that goofy mug clutched in her hand.

I can't quite figure out what the hell it is; some days I think it's a tree, but others it looks like an elf. Who knows. The only thing I know is that it's Christmas themed, and ugly.

She's been going balls-to-the-walls with the holiday shit lately.

I wouldn't have pictured sleek, sexy Meg as a Christmas groupie.

But man, she is over the freaking top. Oddly enough, it's a surprising part of her personality that I find strangely endearing. Since signing as a junior agent with McGinnis, rumor has it that she's a quick learner who soaks up information. You can tell she was born to be a sports agent; I know for a fact she's checked out game tapes from the resource library on the third floor, and that she's on the sidelines for home games. College. Professional. She doesn't just go after the big names. She's hungry and ambitious.

But kind.

Not that I would know about *that*.

I don't know what the hell I ever did to her since we never speak, but she avoids me like the goddamn plague.

I watch as Sheila sits back down in her cubicle then begins applying lipstick using a small mirror. The number of times that woman has hit on our clients is staggering. Seriously mind boggling, and I've often wondered how in the hell she landed a job here. I think most of her clients are geriatric, but still.

Jason's deep timbre cuts in to my train of thought.

…"I think the numbers look really good. Do you think we've spent enough on advertising? The blood bank is reporting another spike in potential bone marrow donors, so that's good, but I'm not sure about the number of volunteers to work at the clinic."

Meg reenters my line of vision, hips swaying in those ridiculous leggings.

"Mmm," I respond, like an asshole because I didn't catch anything he's been saying, and tap a number two pencil on my desktop.

Apparently Meg doesn't know her pants are see-through, the material stretchy, because I got a really good look at her ass this morning when she bent over to grab a file folder off the ground.

Her ass and her pink thong.

Pink.

As in: not a Christmas color.

I wonder what else she's wearing that isn't red and green.

"So. Are you gonna ask her out or what?"

"Huh?" My eyes snap back to Jason's. "Shit, sorry." I have no excuse for not paying attention to every word that's been coming out of his mouth. This man pays my salary and I didn't hear a damn thing he's been saying.

"I asked if you were going to ask her out." He asks the question warily, leaning back in his chair and crossing his arms, making his biceps pop. His biceps. That right there: the reason women like Sheila Dunphy work here. Title chasers.

"Ask who out?"

He rolls his eyes. "Don't make me ask a third time, I know you heard me." He lets out a long, laboring sigh and stares at me like I'm a damn idiot. "The girl in the cubicle across the hall." Another blank stare. "The *Mrs. Clause Wanna-be* with the elf coffee mug and Santa pants?"

Ah, so it is an elf. I freaking knew it.

I give in to the cross examination, and give him a little intel. "Her name is Megan McClaren and I've been trying to figure out what that damn mug is for at least a week."

"You would have known if you talked to her. You don't talk to her, do you?"

"No. She hates me."

Jason laughs, his meaty fist hitting the wooden desk with a loud thud. "Are you fucking kidding me? Adam Roberts? You lead me around by the nuts, and you're afraid of a woman wearing jingle balls."

"It's tinsel, asshole."

"Do you know that for the past three months, every time we've met, you don't hear a damn thing I say? It's a miracle you haven't fucked up my schedule yet. A damn miracle. You have Santa pants on the brain."

"Fine. I thought I was being covert about it, okay? I'd love to ask her out but she doesn't even know my name."

He laughs again. "I *seriously* doubt that."

"Ok, maybe she knows my name. But only because my office is literally across from her cube and it has my name on it."

"Maybe. Orrr maybe she's into you."

"Really." I deadpan. "What gives you that idea?"

"Are you blind? I catch her staring at you through the glass." His grin is shit-eating and confident, just like every other professional athlete that crosses my threshold.

I quirk an irritated eyebrow. "Jason, do me a favor."

"What's that?"

"Cross your arms over your chest again and watch your bicep as you do it."

"Why?" He looks confused by my request. So I say it again.

"Cross your arms over your chest and watch your bicep."

"Okkkkkkay," he says slowly, but he does it. "Why did I just do that?"

"Did you see how that gigantic muscle in your arm flexed when you moved?"

He shrugs, like he doesn't see what I'm getting at.

"That muscle is what she's staring at every time you're here. Not me. Believe me dude, I've been around here long enough to know an office romance isn't just a bad idea for HR purposes. It's also a bad idea because she's not interested."

I freeze when Meg stands, fusses with her desk chair, then takes her seat again. She runs a hand down her hair, fingers brushing through it. It shines under the glaring florescent lights above us. Meg may dress like a crazy cat lady during the month of December, but her face is beautiful. Some days, she piles that hair on top of her head and I can see her long, flawless neck. A neck I'd like to take a bite of—not hard. Maybe just a nip?

I've seen her expressive green eyes sparkle about a client's success.

She's gorgeous. Quirky, real.

Beautiful.

"Oh shit. I've seen that look. You've got it bad." Jason just will not shut up.

"Would you let it go?"

"I bet she has an Ugly Christmas sweater, and she doesn't think it's ugly." He suddenly has an idea, and his face lights up. "Hey! You should see if she wants to come with you to Lindsay's party."

I groan. "I'm not going to that party. No."

"The hell you aren't!" he bellows. "Just because you lost the sweater contest last year doesn't mean you get to puss out of coming."

"I'm not pussing out, asshole, I just refuse to wear the Grinch sweater Addison gave me for Christmas last year."

Addison is Jason's wife.

"You lost the ugly sweater contest—that sweater was your *prize*. You should be cherishing that shit, asshole." He crosses his huge pipes again. "Besides, you have to wear it. It's our family tradition."

I snort. "What tradition? You've been married for like two years."

"Five years in June."

"Whatever. That's not long enough for it to be a tradition."

"It's long enough to me and the Mrs., so it's long enough for you."

I have nothing to say to that, so I don't say anything.

"As the person who fills your bank account, I'm pulling a dick move and demanding that you come to Lindsay's party. Ask the girl to come with you."

He stands up, stretches, and moves to the door.

"I guess this meeting is over?"

"You can't keep your head out of that cubicle over there so there's no point anyway. I'll catch you later man." He turns around and points right at me. "Don't be late for the party, asshole."

"Fine."

"Seven o'clock."

"I know what time it starts."

He sniggers and begins walking away. But then he stops, moonwalks backwards, and lays a hand on my doorjamb.

"And don't forget the sweater."

My eyes drift to Meg's cubicle. She's watching Jason saunter down the carpeted hallway, a smile lighting up her entire face.

A smile that's wiped from her mouth when she looks over and see's me watching.

CHAPTER 2

"My lack of an office romance is holding me back professionally."
MEG

I love the mall at Christmas time.

The hustle and bustle that normal people can't stand. The smell of the food court, especially the cinnamon buns. The baked pretzels and cookies. Let's not forget the music, decorations, and the children waiting in line to meet Santa. There's something magical about a child's faith that a hired employee can make all their dreams come true.

Poor things.

One of my favorite parts of the Santa shop are the pictures of terror stricken and crying kids that end up on Social media. I know, I know, that kind of makes me a jerk, because I should feel sympathy but I don't. I can't help it; those pictures are absolutely hysterical.

So here I am—no, no, not scouring the mall for the perfect gift. Nope, not me. I'm on the prowl for another kind of perfect: the perfect dress.

I sigh, not familiar with this mall or where to find this unicorn outfit.

"Can I help you find something, darlin? You look lost." A thick Texas drawl comes out of nowhere and scares the bejeezus out of me.

I turn to see a woman with the biggest hair I've ever seen in my life—a beehive, I think they call it— looking at me. She has more make-up on than Tammy Fay Baker (God Bless her soul), and she's chewing gum like a longhorn chews on cud. Oh god, did I just make a Texan reference?

Of course, I have no room to judge her. I'm wearing see-through Santa leggings.

Plus, this woman has a huge, inviting smile on her face, and I recognize a friendly face when I see one.

"Yes ma'am." There I go again, sounding Texan. "I need an outfit for my office Christmas party."

She chews twice and snaps her gum. "What kind of outfit are ya lookin' for?"

I shake my head. "I'm thinking classy. Fun. Maybe something sparkly?"

Her smile widens. "Well, yer in the right place, honey! We specialize in sparkle."

I must look terrified as she takes me by the arm and drags me into her store.

She laughs. "Oh don't be afraid, darlin'. Rhonda will take good care of you. I'm Rhonda, by the by." She links her arm through mine and guides me toward the back of the store. "Here at The Dress Stable, we have everything you'll ever need in office dress. Dresses, pants, shirts, chaps, … you name it. Do I detect a Midwestern accent?"

Chaps? Did she seriously say *chaps*?

As she shows me around, all I can think is, *I have never seen more leather fringe in my life*. Rhinestones. Turquoise. And does everyone own a pair of chaps in this town? They're everywhere.

Am I missing something by not having any? And how can I get my hands on a pair of those pink studded cowboy boots?

Or maybe I stumbled into the wrong place…

"Just look around and jingle if you need anything," Rhonda says. "I'll be going through some new inventory that just came in."

As she struts her way back to the front, wearing a blue version of the boots I have my eye on, I turn my attention to the racks around me. Plaid studded shirts, western wear, and denim as far as the eye can see. But then I walk further, and further, past the shoes and boots and hats and stumble into some of the most beautiful dresses I've ever seen. Solid wrap dresses made out of the finest cotton. Silky shifts.

Of course, they're displayed with cowboy boots, but they're perfect.

I grab one dress, then another, until I have an armload. Stumble to the curtained dressing room. Peel off my red sweater without getting caught in the Christmas lights strung across Rudolph's crochet horns. Leggings. Shoes.

I go to work trying everything on.

Unfortunately…thirty minutes and twelve outfits later, I'm no closer to finding a dress than I was when I started.

"Rhonda?" I call from the fitting room when I'm done re-hanging my last cast off. "Thanks so much for your help. I appreciate it—and I loved a few of these, they just didn't fit right."

I shrug helplessly, disappointed and tired, heading back toward the mall.

"Darlin! Wait!" she calls out. "I meant to bring this to you, but I got sidetracked by the new shoes." She reaches behind the counter. "I found this in Christmas red." She winks, revealing a simple wrap dress. Rich red, thick fabric—it's the perfect color. Better yet, it has tiny rhinestones lining the pleats. "Want to give one more a try?"

Eager, all I can do is nod as she hands me the hanger.

"Size six, I reckon? That's what you wear, right?" I caress the silky material. "Well, go try it on. Scoot, scoot!" She shoos me into a dressing room, practically climbing inside with me.

Stripping off my clothes once again, my heart starts pounding. The material feels *amazing* against my bare skin. More amazing than my Santa leggings. I'm almost afraid to turn around and look in the mirror.

But I do.

I gasp.

It's perfect.

There's enough sparkle to make it festive, but it's classy, not gaudy. It fits me like a second skin on my upper torso, flaring at the waist. The belt surrounding my waist falls down the pleated skirt.

"Rhonda!" I screech, whipping the curtain wide open. "This is the dress!"

"Just as I thought. Rhonda knows dresses, darling, and that one was made for you. Here. Take a gander at what I found to go with it." She holds up a pair of black, sling backs. The leather is glossy and butter soft, the heel a sexy three inches. "Try these on. They're on sale." She leans in close and whispers, "Last season."

I do as she says, removing my ballet flat and sliding my foot into the black shoes.

I look down at the price tag, and groan.

"Now, I know it's a lot of money, honey, but you can't put a price on this kind of perfection."

Well, technically you can, I want to say. Two hundred and some odd change.

But I bite my lip and crunch the numbers in my head to include the tax. Christmas always means more money out of my pocket. But I really want to make an impression tomorrow.

Tomorrow, I'm going to *talk* to Adam.

And I don't want to do it in a glowing tee shirt and candy cane leggings.

I want to look *sexy*.

"Ok." I yank the tag off the dress, handing it and my credit card to Rhonda "Ring it up before I change my mind. The shoes, too." I squeeze my eyes shut and then add, "Don't tell me the total!"

She bounces, and her hair bounces along with her boobs. "This is so excitin'. You won't regret this! And! You just helped me make my quota for the month."

She doesn't hesitate to charge my credit card a month's worth of groceries while I return to the fitting room, get dressed again in my street clothes, and collect my things.

As much as it cost me, I actually feel good about my purchases. I'm giddy.

Excited.

As I round the corner, I stop dead in my tracks.

Adam.

He doesn't see me, but I definitely see him. I fiddle with the garment bag slung over my arm like a rag doll, watching as he stands at the entrance of a toy store, staring down at the floor. At the remote controlled cars zooming around the tile floor. Hand on his chin, it looks like he's debating buying them.

My heart sinks.

Of course he has kids. Which probably means he's married. It makes sense. A guy that successful and attractive is bound to be off the market—I was a fool to think otherwise.

I'm surprised I haven't heard anything about it in the office, but then again, I'm new and just getting to know people. The only one who tells me anything gossipy is Sheila, and I only believe half of what she tells me.

Feeling defeated, the weight of my dress weighing heavier with every step, I make my way through the crowd. To the only man who can make me feel better this time of year.

Santa Clause.

* * *

ADAM

I HATE the mall at Christmas time.

I can't freaking stand the hustle and bustle here to begin with, and now the crowds are just stifling. The smell of the food court is making me ill, especially the cinnamon buns. The line for the unhealthy baked pretzels and cookies make me cringe. And can we not forget the music, decorations, and the children waiting in line to meet Santa? It's pitiful that children put their faith in a hired employee, thinking he can make all their dreams come true.

Poor things.

Seriously, its the middle of the week. What the hell are people doing here? Doesn't anyone shop online shop anymore? I mean, go back home and use your damn computers like regular people!

I'm such a damn hypocrite.

I can only blame myself for forgetting about the Ugly Christmas Sweater party Jason's making me attend in a few days. Which means I need gifts for his two kids.

I don't have a fucking clue what kids play with these days, so I was grateful for the pretty blond cashier's help picking out a few remote controlled cars. She swore up and down they were perfect for both a three-year-old and twelve-year-old.

Two cars. Boom, done.

Wrap 'em up.

I was, however, less grateful for her very obvious advances toward me.

Three months ago I would have flirted back in a heartbeat. Three months ago, I didn't have a certain dark haired, junior agent on my mind twenty-four hours a day. I have no idea why Meg has me tied up in knots, but it's starting to piss me off. It's not like we ever work on any accounts together—we should be able to at least be friends.

Hell, these days, I only have one account to work on, so any conflict of interest wouldn't be a concern. But the few times I've said, "How about those Cowboys?" she's bolted from the break room faster than, well, a college football running back.

So instead of getting to know her, I spend my days glancing out my door to watch her work.

What do they call them these days? Creepers? That's what I've turned into.

A creeper.

Smooth, I know.

"Oomph!"

I rub my shin and stare at the pint-sized person who's just plowed right into me, almost knocking me on my ass. As I regain my bearings, I glare down at the kid—a boy, maybe five years old. And he looks…well, he looks kind of scared.

"Hey, you okay there buddy?" I ask him, looking around to see who he's with. Where are his parents?

He just shakes his head.

"Are you hurt? Did I hurt you when you bumped into me?"

He shakes his head again.

Ok, so this isn't going well.

"So if you aren't hurt, why aren't you okay?"

The sniffles begin and I cringe. Yeah. I cringe.

There are few things I can't stand:

1. Shopping at the mall
2. Shopping at the mall during the holidays. Any holiday.
3. Crying children.

Put the three things together, and you have the recipe to why I'd rather spend the night in a one room cabin with my creepy Uncle Frederick after a long night of drinking. Don't ask for details, just trust me.

"I can't find my mom," the kid mumbles, on the brink of having a meltdown.

"Okay, okay buddy, don't start crying." I'm sure I sound harsh, but seriously—if he starts to wail, I'm out. I don't care if he's lost.

Fine, I care, I'm just not equipped to handle this. Where is security when you need them?

"Where did you last see her?"

"In the store."

Good thing the mall is full of stores, I think uncharitably.

"Ok, let's try this again. Where were you guys going when you got separated?"

"Over there." He points towards the main thoroughfare, where hundreds of people are milling about, with six different walkways going this way and that. Basically a veritable treasure trove if you're looking to disappear.

I stare blankly at him for a few seconds.

He is obviously not the brightest Christmas bulb on the tree. Then again, he only looks five-years-old.

"Okay, last time before I give up and ditch you on a bench somewhere. Do you know where you were trying to go?"

He nods. "We were going to see Santa."

Ah! I clap my hands and rub them together.

Now that's information I can work with.

"That's a good place to start. I betcha she's there waiting for you. Come on kid. I'll walk you over there."

Instead of following me, like I assume he's going to, he narrows his eyes and puts his hands on his hips. "But you're a stranger."

"Look kid, you ran into me and almost started crying because you're lost. I'm heading over to Santa anyway because I parked my car in that direction. If you want to walk with me and try to find your mom, you can. If not, you can park your little butt on that bench over there until security finds you. What's it gonna be?"

He thinks for a few seconds, obviously sizing me up. "Fine. But if you try any funny business, I'm telling Santa."

I'd laugh, except that's a pretty serious threat coming from a kindergardener.

"Fine. But if *you* try anything funny, I'll tell Santa myself. And you don't have money to buy your own toys like I do."

His eyes widen momentarily before he takes my hand in his. It's sticky and sweaty and pretty fucking gross. But what am I gonna do?

"What's your name?" he asks me.

"Adam Roberts. What's yours?"

"Clark."

I snort. "Clark? Like Clark Griswold?"

He looks at me like I'm stupid. "Like Gable."

"How do you know who Clark Gable is?"

He shrugs. "My mom likes old movies."

"Makes sense."

"What's in the bag?" he asks gesturing towards my bag of gift for the Harts.

"Remote controlled cars. I have to give some gifts to a client's kids."

"What's a client?"

"Someone I work for at my job."

"Why do you have to give his kids presents?"

"It's good business."

"My dad says clients can buy their *own* presents."

"Your dad probably doesn't have any clients that make several million bucks a year."

Before we even round the corner where I know Santa is holding court, Clark releases my hand and takes off running as fast as his tiny sneakers can carry him. "Mom! Mom!" He shouts, throwing his arms around some woman's legs.

She looks down at him like she didn't even realize he was

missing. No wonder the kid seemed savvy on stranger danger. I'm probably not his first encounter, or his first time being lost.

I'm turning toward the parking garage when a familiar red sweater catches my attention.

It's Meg.

She's wearing the same thing she had on at the office and holding a goofy Christmas ornament shaped purse. And she's sitting on Santa's lap, smiling at the creepy old dude.

I'm not normally one to feel jealous.

I've never been that guy, even when I'm dating someone and it's serious. But for some inexplicable reason, I'm jealous now.

Jealous of Santa Clause. Of Jolly old St. Nick.

What the fuck is wrong with me?

I watch, like the creeper we've established I am, as she chats with the fat bastard for a few minutes longer. As much of a scrooge as I am, the smile on her face makes *me* smile. Maybe I could wait around and talk to her for a while? Maybe I could invite her for coffee? Invite her to the Ugly Sweater Party?

Maybe, maybe, maybe.

Goddammit Roberts, make a fucking move.

As she jumps up off Santa's lap, I watch him check out her ass —the one with his face plastered all over it—and if there weren't children around, I might have words with Kris Kringle.

Instead, I start to approach as Meg pays for her overpriced photo with the pervert. But before I can get to her, a tall, broad chested man with chiseled features reaches her first and kisses her on the cheek. She looks over at him and, much to my dismay, her face lights up. She obviously knows him and worse, *likes* him.

I should have figured.

A woman with her spunk and tenacity would obviously be taken. As they walk away together, he takes the garment bag she's holding, and I feel like an idiot for pining over a woman an entire three months without ever taking the time to find out any real information on her.

Obviously, I'm losing my touch.

"I need to get laid," I mutter loudly, running my hand down my face. The woman standing next to me gives a horrified look, and steps away. "Don't worry. Not by *you.*"

Her jaw drops in indignation before she quickly grabs her child's hand and huffs, stomping away. I shake my head. Maybe some intern will get drunk and horny at the office party tomorrow night and I'll get lucky.

Because the rest of my luck seems to have run out.

CHAPTER 3

I love my peppermint mocha.

I love my red plastic holiday cup—the one I get every year from the coffee chain in town (you know the one). Every year, I look forward to seeing what color cup they're going to release for the Holidays.

They're so festive, and always get me in the Christmas spirit.

I'm holding one now as I click open an email, scanning the contents and furrowing my brow. This entire email…none of it makes sense. Setting the cup down, I guide it across my desk so it will be safe from spilling, and widen my arms so I can respond to this message with—

"Now what the fuck are you wearing?"

"Good morning to you, too, Sheila," I say as kindly as I can, given her rude greeting. Seriously, some people.

"Yeah, yeah, morning, blah, blah, blah. What the fuck are you wearing?"

I swivel around in my chair to glare at her, but she is once again putting lipstick on and not paying attention, so I can't even level her with an angry scowl. "Why are you so worried about my clothes?"

"Because I was gonna win *ten* bucks from Frank in Human Resources if you're wearing an ugly Christmas sweater today." She glances up at me and notices my shocked expression. "What? You didn't think you could dress like Rudolph threw up on you every day for a month and not expect people to take bets, did you?"

For the one hundredth time, "I'm being festive!"

"I'm not complaining. Whatever it is you're doing, keep doing it because you're making me a lot of money." She looks me up and down again skeptically. "I'm not sure if that counts as an ugly Christmas sweater, though."

"First of all," she rolls her eyes as I begin speaking. "It's a tee shirt. Just because the picture on it is an ugly sweater, doesn't make it an ugly sweater. So you lose. Second of all, it's cute and fun."

"It's not cute, Meg. It's ugly. Hence, why it's designed to look like an ugly sweater. And don't tell Franklin I lost. From far away, he probably can't tell the difference. He's not wearing his glasses today, so mums the word."

I press a few fingers to my temple to ward off an impending headache. "You're horrible, and distracting. I need to get back to work."

"…Says the woman who wore a shirt that *literally* had bells on it last week." Sheila snickers.

My head shoots up. "Hey! I said I was sorry for jingling all day. Are you ever going to let that go?"

She crosses her arms stubbornly. "Only if you stay across the room from Franklin today."

"Fine." Sometimes I hate working here.

Sigh.

No that's not true.

I love it.

But sometimes I wish this was college, and I could put in a request to change dorm rooms—I mean, cubicles—so I could neighbor with someone less insulting, less into making bets, less...gold digging. What I would love is for her to show me how things get done around here. How to climb the ladder. How to use the tools and online resources McGinnis has downloaded onto each of our computers.

Take this contract in front of me, for example: I've been writing it for a potential client since yesterday, had several questions, and Sheila has been no help whatsoever.

I hate bugging my interoffice messenger buddy, but at this point, I'm not sure I have much of a choice.

See, McGinnis Agency has a unique system to help newbies—like me—get through the learning curve. It's an inter-office messaging system called IOM. Basically it's a clever acronym for "Inter-Office Messaging," because no one around here was creative enough to call it something fancier.

When you open IOM, you have a list of departments. When you click on the department, it brings up a list of registered staff members, management, and executives who have signed-up to mentor anyone with questions.

Here's the kicker: they're corporate assigned usernames so it's completely anonymous.

It's weird and takes some getting used to.

But fantastic.

New employees—like me—are able to contact *anyone* in *any* department with a client related subject you might normally be too intimidated to approach the department head about; there's no stigma if you're ignorant on the issue you're researching. McGinnis was built on team work, for team members, and models the entire corporation on that principle.

So the IOM, in a nutshell, is mentoring.

No one on the IOM gets accolades for assisting. No one gets penalized if they choose not to mentor, because the program is voluntary. Everyone is on equal footing. No one knows who you are, so feedback is usually unbiased. Which is great, because when you're working in a cut-throat field like this one—where every agent is gunning for the next big contract—equality and anonymity is crucial.

At least, that's the idea.

So that's where I turn now, because Sheila sucks and is the least helpful person within grabbing distance. Better yet, I found someone with some contract negotiation background, and they've helped me tremendously as I try to perfect this tedious work.

Man, woman—I have no idea. But they've been amazing.

Clicking through the IOM database, I see the icon for *Mentor-Team259* lit up in green.

Good, who ever MentorTeam259 is, they're here and online. They're also one of my favorite go-to mentors in this department. Whoever it is.

I quickly type out a greeting.

Me: *Good morning. When you're situated this morning and have had some coffee, do you have a few minutes? I need to pick your brain about a contract discrepancy.*

They respond within seconds. Excellent.

MentorTeam259: *No problem. I'm not quite caffeinated yet, but I have time right now. Hit me with it.*

Me: *Great. I'll cut to the chase. I'm running into several questionable demands by a rather new client, and I'm not sure where to categorize them in relation to the standard compensation package.*

MentorTeam259: *What kind of questionable demands? Like a new car every year, or hookers after each Victory?*

Me: *THEY ASK FOR THINGS LIKE THAT?!?!!? Sorry I'm yelling, but THEY ASK FOR THINGS LIKE THAT? I think I just scared my cubicle mate.*

MentorTeam259: *Lol! No. Well, yes. Sometimes. My point though is gauging how ridiculous these demands actually are.*

Me: *Please don't do that to me, lol. It made me both afraid of what I'm about to get myself into and delighted about the drama that could arise. Obviously I have a very boring personal laugh. Ha ha.*

MentorTeam259: *Ha! Somehow I doubt that. But. Getting back to the point; Typically, if it's anything beyond the standard compensation package, we use an addendum noted at the end of the contract. There should be a link on how to create one in the system. Keyword search: Comp Standard. It should be in the Appendix file.*

Me: *There's an Appendix file? I'm assuming the Appendix file is where all other files are hidden.*

MentorTeam259: *You're lucky you have me if they haven't trained you on this already.*

Me: *Sorry. You're right, I haven't been trained on this. Now I'm wondering what else I haven't learned. It's either that, or the fact I spent last night drinking wine with my next door neighbor. Cheap wine.*

MentorTeam259: *Sounds more exciting than my night. I spent it wrapping Christmas presents and getting ready for a party I don't want to go to.*

Me: *A holiday party? My favorite!*

MentorTeam259: *I'd rather take a hard pass. Stay in and watch the NFL season ticket.*

Me: *You just gave me a clue about yourself.*

MentorTeam259: *Are you collecting evidence for something?*

Me: *I was going to say 'I'm going to assume you're a man', but then I remembered I have the NFL season ticket, too.*

MentorTeam259: *Ah, so now I have some information on you— you're a woman.*

Me: *Don't tell anyone, it's a secret. LOL*

MentorTeam259: *Fine, I'll let you in on my secret: I'm not a woman either.*

Me: *Wait. Are we going to get in trouble for this? I thought the IOM was confidential.*

MentorTeam259: *It's possible we'll get in trouble, yes, but I'm going to blame you, so...*

Me: *Do you take bribes?*

MentorTeam259: *Lack of confidentiality, BRIBES—we are entering some seriously dangerous water here...*

Me: *Oh Jeez, this isn't even the strangest conversation I've had today. And it's only 8:00*

MentorTeam259: *You mean you've had stranger conversations this week? Do tell.*

Me: *My friend Tabitha Thompson is a romance author and likes to fill me in every morning on what she's working on. Use your imagination for a second about what we talk about (dot dot dot).*

MentorTeam259: *Uh, what's the (dot dot dot)? It sounds like I need to know more. Is she getting romance advice from you?*

Me: *Why, do YOU need some romance advice?*

I hold my breath, waiting for his reply.

MentorTeam259: *Shit yes.*

MentorTeam259: *Crap. There's also no profanity on the IOM.*

Me: *Seriously? Then we're both in trouble, because I'm pretty sure I swore in a message to MentorTeam001 last week. Not to mention, I know half of YOUR identity already. Male. Gainfully employed. Anti-Holidays...*

MentorTeam259: *I never said I was Anti-Holiday—Just anti holiday PARTY...*

Me: *Why?*

MentorTeam259: *I hate going to those alone.*

Me: *So you're single?*

I perk up, then cringe, having asked such a personal question. I sound so nosey. And desperate.

Me: *Sorry, I should not have asked that. You don't have to answer.*

MentorTeam259: *No, it's okay. Yes, I'm single. Yes, I hate going to parties alone. No, I'm not online dating.*

Me: *It's like you were reading my mind. You've never done online dating? Why? It's so fun!*

MentorTeam259: *Long story. Also, did I mention these IOM conversations get randomly screened by the IT Department? We've probably already said too much personal shit, broken about three rules, and I've just used profanity for the second time in ten minutes.*

Me: *Shit, shit, shit. Now we're both in trouble when the IOM Police come to track us down.*

MentorTeam259: *Would you go to IOM Prison for me?*

Me: *No man left behind. Have you ever seen the movie The Santa Clause? The elves break him out of prison using tinsel and jet packs? I'd total do that. I have some you know.*

MentorTeam259: *HOLY SHIT, YOU HAVE JET PACKS?*

Me: *No, I have TINSEL.*

MentorTeam259: *Oh. That's not as exciting.*

Me: *LOL. It can be.*

Oh my god, I did not just say that! I quickly type out a, *I guess I should let you get back to work...* and hit send.

I don't really want to end this, though. I want to keep chatting. Whoever MentorTeam259 is...he sounds fun. I picture him to be kind of dorky. Smart. Probably with glasses, like my friend Daphne's boyfriend, Dexter.

I bet MentorTeam259 is cute. Shoot, I'm already half attracted to his online personality.

I glance up to the office where Adam sits at his computer, head down, a small smile playing at the corner of his mouth. He picks up his coffee mug—a plain white one with words across the front that I can't read from here, and takes a long sip. Licks his lips and sets it down.

Leans back in his chair, clasping his hands behind his neck and staring at his monitor. I can see him thinking from here, brows furrowed in concentration. A moment passes, then another.

He releases his hands, stretches, then sets back to typing as I watch, cheeks warm and something strange fluttering inside my chest. My heart is beating wildly, the melody to *All I Want for*

Christmas is You playing in the background in my cubicle through the speakers on my monitor, when my IMO pings with a new message.

MentorTeam259: *This is completely unethical and against policy, but…*

My heartbeat speeds up, if that were possible.

MentorTeam259: *You know what? Nevermind. I shouldn't be asking.*

My shoulders sag.

I raise my head, glancing toward Adam's office, eyes widening when our gazes collide. Embarrassed, I jerk my head back to my computer screen. Before I can think twice, I type out another question to MentorTeam259.

Me: *You should totally give the whole online dating thing a shot. You have an amazing online personality.*

MentorTeam259: *You think?*

Me: *Oh yeah. I don't know you personally, obviously, but I can tell you're pretty great.*

This is not a dating website, Meg! I remind myself so I don't get too unprofessional.

Me: *Are you going to the Office Party tonight?*

MentorTeam259: *Yes. You?*

Me: *Yes.*

Okay, now what?

MentorTeam259: *Crazy thought…if you're willing to go down in a blaze of glory.*

Me: *You have my full attention.*

The over-imaginative part of me can almost hear Mentor-Team259 clearing his throat uncomfortably. Pulling at the collar of his shirt, loosening his tie. Like Adam is doing right now. It's a red power tie, and he's tugging it at the knot, unbuttoning that first button of his starched baby blue dress shirt.

He cracks his fingers above his keyboard, then goes in.

MentorTeam259: *Meet me at the Christmas tree tonight that's always by the Reception desk in the lobby. They decorate it with blue ornaments every year, and there's a white star at the top that never lights up. You can't miss it.*

That's the thing about the lobby in this building. It's massive, completely surrounded by glass, with twenty-four-foot-high ceilings, sky rocketing beams, and huge, full grown potted trees. Massive crystal chandelier gleam overhead.

Definitely large and grand enough to host a company Holiday party.

Me: Okay. Yes!! 8:30?

I'm trying to contain my enthusiasm, but I just can't help adding those two exclamation points.

MentorTeam259: *Great. See you then.*

It's on the tip of my fingers to type *It's a Date!* so instead, I go with: *I look forward to meeting the man who's gotten me out of a few conundrums.*

I inwardly cringe. I should have messaged Tabitha about this; she would know the perfect thing to say and she sure as hell wouldn't use the word conundrum.

MentorTeam259: *Let me know if you get stuck any more with the contract.*

Me: *Sounds good.*

I log off and get back to work. I have no idea who MentorTeam259 is, but he sounds nice. Funny. I'm looking forward to possibly having an actual office friend, and try desperately not to think of this as a blind date.

But fail miserably.

Sheila reappears over my cubicle. "Did you get an actual outfit for tonight or just another ugly shirt?"

I sigh, spinning in my chair to face her. She's standing with her arms folded along the top of my walls, steaming hot mug of something in her hands. The steam rises up, and she blows on it, a dreamy expression on her face. Doubtless daydreaming about all the men she's going to hustle at tonight's party.

"No. But I did go shopping and got a gorgeous dress," I can't stop myself from gushing. Just a little. "Probably paid too much money, but I like it." Then I add, "I think you'll actually be proud of me."

"Yay!" Sheila claps, almost dropping her mug. It's brown and plain, and not Christmasy at all, so it wouldn't be a total loss if she did. "Are you going to let Deborah do your hair and make up? I bet her *five* bucks you'd do the smart thing and go shopping, but she didn't believe me. So she loses."

I cock a brow. "Sheila. You have a serious gambling problem— you do know that, right?"

"Only when it comes to your poor sense in fashion." She takes another few sips of coffee, and I suspect there might be something other than coffee in it. Something much. *Stronger.* "And you've already won me next month's car payment, so I'm not about to stop betting on my winningest horse."

Am I the horse in this scenario? Awesome.

I drop my head to my desk and groan. Why? *Why* of all the people in this office do I have to be neighbors with this one? Why not Caroline, who's cube is four away? She brings her neighbors cookies, and has a string of festive, colorful lights above her cabinets. Or better yet, Mark, the quiet computer nerd across the narrow hall. He might be a mute, but he's polite and keeps to himself. And, I notice he has a Santa bobble head on a stack of Sports Management manuals, so he can't be all that bad...

"Remember," Sheila is saying now, voice authoritative. "A few of us gals are meeting at 5:30 to primp. We heard Norman Hayward is going to be here this year and I want to have Deborah contour my wrinkles." Mr. Hayward is the VP COO of our company and is recently divorced from the third Mrs. Hayward. It sounds like Sheila is gunning to be the fourth. "Meet us in the sixth floor Ladies' washroom. I smuggled some bourbon in my purse so we'll start the party a little early."

Washroom? Bourbon? Hard pass.

"Thanks for the invitation. I'll think about it." I give her a polite smile and brush away a few loose strands of hair from my lips. It's sticking to the North Pole Peppermint Chapstick I just applied.

"5:30," she says again with a nod. "We'll doll you up real nice."

Oh, I just *bet* you will.

* * *

ADAM

DAMN, whoever McGinnis983 is, she's funny. She makes me laugh every damn time we chat, and although a small knot of guilt forms in my stomach from having broken the company's confidentiality agreement—and about four other policies—I'm not sorry I get to find out who she is.

Even if she's a troll up on the eighth floor who always sends me an inter-office memo when I take one too many steno pads from the supply room. Then at least I'll have a face to go with the name. Or, in this case, the Screen Name.

Fine. I'm secretly hoping who ever she is, she's not the office hag.

I'm hoping she's as sexy as she is clever.

I'm still thinking about McGinnis983 when I glance through the wall of windows that make up my office, to Meg's small desk.

Her open cubicle entrance faces mine, so I can see inside without any effort or obstructions. I'm able to freely study her profile and the long, brown hair falling in silky waves. Her sweater is red, and though I can't see the front, I'd bet money that's it's got one of those butt ugly designs on it.

Speaking of bets, it's common knowledge that more than a few people have made Meg the prime target of the office betting pool, another thing that's frowned upon by Human Resources around here. Given that our profession is professional athletes, and betting on sports is *illegal*, the fact that our employees are betting within the office is deplorable.

Meg shifts in her seat, and I'm given a full frontal of her sweater. I was right; it's fucking ugly.

Red, with a quilted sweater sewn onto the front, it's an ugly sweater…sweater? Bright, plastic lights, strung across the front of it that I *bet* have a battery pack somewhere that lights them up.

Shit. Now I'm doing it.

Meg stands, pulling the sweater down over her ass. Plucks at the fabric of her green and blue plaid leggings. Plops back down in her seat. Begins shuffling files around on her desk, occasionally jotting notes down on a pink sticky note pad. I've noticed her doing that a lot; jotting notes. Little post it's are everywhere in her cubicle—on her monitor, on the two gray shelves, on her file cabinet.

I wonder what they all say.

I wonder what she's thinking when she looks up, into my office.

I try to smile, but it comes out as a grimace, and she quickly looks back down, but not before I see her lips saying, "Oh god," and she spins her chair away from me.

Great. Now she thinks I'm a freak.

Which…I won't lie. I've tried to look up information on her. Personal shit that I thought maybe I could use to strike up a conversation with. Shit, I've even tried looking her up in the office directory, then stopped when I felt stalkery. The last thing I want is to invade her privacy by creeping on her.

After awhile, Meg visibly relaxes, concentrating on her work. From here I can see her biting down on her lower lip and scrunching up her nose every few minutes. It's sexy adorable.

Yeah. Definitely sexy adorable.

I wonder if McGinnis983 will be sexy adorable, too.

CHAPTER 4

"I want to break the company's HR policy with you."
MEG

With a trembling hand, I smooth down my long hair, it having mercifully fallen into loose waves after being in a top knot all day. The finishing touches on my make-up are done; I managed a smoky eye without looking like a raccoon, my contouring artfully applied—for once. Instead of false eyelashes, which were sure to tear off and get stuck to my cheeks, the mascara I found at the mall elongated my lashes so it looks like I am. Lips glossy.

I run a palm down the front of my new dress, flattening out the pleats—if possible, the dress is better than I remember. When I pulled it out of the garment bag last night to iron out the wrinkles, the cool fabric slipped smoothly between my fingers before I finally slipped it on.

The dress looks even better today than it did yesterday. Feels amazing.

The shoes feel even more comfortable.

I feel pretty.

I twirl, catching my reflection in the mirror.

Gathering the clothes I wore to work, I check the time—I'm a little late, but only casually—shove everything into a tote with the North Pole printed on it, and drop it off in my cubicle. Once I reach the elevator banks, clicking across the white marble floors on my new high heels, I give the down button a gentle push with a red polished nail. There's a small candy cane painted on my pinky finger, and I smile when it catches my eye with a flirty little wink.

The elevator opens slowly, and I can already hear the notes of music wafting up from the lobby below. Obviously, as a new employee, I haven't been to an office Christmas party before, so I'm curious if they actually get as wild as Sheila claims. If it gets crowded with clients, owners, and coaches. I know first hand how prone Sheila is to exaggerations, so I'm interested to see who will be crowded around the bar tonight.

And of course, my meeting with MentorTeam259.

The elevator still hasn't arrived, so even though I know it's pointless, I poke at the down button again. It's been slow to arrive before, but this is ridiculous, even with a throng of people forming in the lobby, barely anyone would be using them to cause them to stall.

I tilt my head, watching the numbers lower. It's coming from the higher floors, gradually making it's way down. Thirteenth floor. *Pause.*

Tenth floor.

Ninth.

Pause.

Eight.

Ding!

Finally, the elevator slides open and I hop on, immediately reaching for the panel board. Give the lobby a poke. Wait for the doors to slide closed, facing them. When they're in place, I step back, leaning against the cool wall, stunned to realize there's actually another person tucked away in the corner, head down, on his phone.

My eyes begin the slow decent from the tips of his shiny leather shoes, his long legs. Tapered waist. Broad chest...

The lights suddenly shut off.

I stand stunned, in the pitch black car.

"What's happening?" I ask quietly. Or was it a whisper?

The entire elevator is pitch black. Not even the emergency light on the control panel is lit up.

"Come on, answer your damn phone," the man says. And he has a low, baritone voice. Okay, so maybe being trapped in this elevator won't be so bad.

He slams what sounds like a phone back down into it's metal box.

"Shit."

"Was that the red emergency phone?"

"Yup." He hesitates, then asks, "You okay?"

"I'm fine," I answer, thinking how weird it is not being able to see the person I'm talking to. I can't quite figure out where I'm supposed to look. "Why did you hang up? Should we call them back?"

He sighs. "The *last* time this happened—"

"—What do you mean *last* time?"

"About two years ago, a few people got stuck here a few hours."

"How many? Do you remember?"

"I mean...not to alarm you, but you asked." He clears his throat, the sound reverberating in the small space. "It was overnight."

I gasp. Fine, it's more like a squeak. "Overnight! What took them so long to get rescued?"

"Not sure?" The voice says. "From what I understand, they were the last ones leaving for the night. The next morning, when someone punched the call button, the elevator just started moving again."

"No one ever answered the emergency phone?"

"Apparently he'd already gone home for the night."

"Just like now," I whisper. "He's probably down at the party and can't hear his phone over the band."

The voice chuckles. I like the sound. It makes me feel tingly, which is utterly ridiculous. This person is a nameless, faceless stranger.

Whoever is sharing this ride with me grunts. "He's probably taking advantage of the free booze at the party right now—just what we need; a drunk rescue worker."

"I've heard more people talk about this free alcohol. Is it really that good? Or is it good because it's free?" I chuckle despite myself.

"Both, I guess. But there's a shit ton of it, so…"

"Great. I'll be throwing them back after this ordeal for sure."

We hang out in silence a little longer, listening to the sounds of the party below us. I'm not sure what song is being played, because the bass of the band creates a hollow sound inside the elevator, making it impossible to distinguish any words.

"Well," I finally say with a sign. "What shall we do while we wait?"

He rustles around before he speaks, his voice carrying from a different angle now. "Cop a squat. Pull up a seat. Make yourself comfortable." Pause. "This could be a while."

ADAM

"THIS COULD BE AWHILE." The woman repeats.

I have no idea who it is, but she works on my floor and is wearing a red dress and sexy, black heels. I saw at least that much when she hopped into the elevator. The long, toned legs. The swish and sparkle of her skirt.

I wish now that I hadn't had my head buried in my cell phone —the phone rendered fucking useless from lack of satellite signal in this stuffy car—I'd just been lifting my eyes when the lights blacked out.

"I mean, not to be a drag, but we might as well sit." Shit, she's wearing a dress. "Are you okay sitting on the floor in that dress?"

"It's okay. I can always take it to the dry cleaners." A sniffle in the dark. "Not to be a downer, but it's brand new. I bought it special for tonight." A long, heavy sigh. "At least it's comfortable, right?"

"What does it look like?" Shit, why did I just ask that? Like I care what her dress looks like.

I can hear her smiling in the dark. "It's Christmas red. Well, technically that's not the name of it, but that's what I'm calling it. It wraps around the waist, and the belt has the smallest, glistening rhinestones on it. Just like the ones sewn into the pleats."

"I didn't see it," I admit. "I just saw the button when you walked in, but I'm sure its real...uh. Pretty."

Probably sexy, too, judging by her legs alone.

"*It is.*"

"Well, I'm sure we'll be out of here soon enough. I doubt we'll miss the *entire* party." Just most of it, unless we have to spend the night—but I keep that part to myself.

"I hope not. I was on my way to meet someone."

"Yeah, me too." My stomach growls then, and thank god for the pitch black because I blush a bright red, something I swear I haven't done in years. "Do you happen to have any food in your purse? Apparently, I'm starving."

I hear the snap on her purse click, then some riffling. "I always keep a protein bar with me. Want to split it? Or should we ration it into small pieces, just in case."

The crinkling of a plastic wrapper tickles my ears.

I laugh. "I think we're safe just splitting it down the middle." I hold out my hand in the dark, and then remember she can't see me. "I'm over here, holding my hand out like the begger that I am."

"Hold on, let me find you." A hand grazes my arm. Latches on, feeling down my forearm. Slowly then, sliding the rest of the way down. "Um. There you are, haha." She coughs, fingers feeling for my open palm. The protein bar gets placed in the center. "I hope that's half."

I lift it to my mouth, taking a bite. "Mmm, tastes like filet."

Whoever she is, she thinks I'm funny, and laughs. "Mine tastes like…" She chews, and I can hear her swallow dramatically. "Blueberries and cream. Wait. Now it tastes like mash potatoes!"

"Charlie and the Chocolate Factory? Good one—real clever."

"Thanks."

"Did you just wink at me in the dark?"

She laughs again. "No! Why would you ask me that, weirdo."

I consider her question, shrugging. "It just seems like it would have been an appropriate time to wink at someone."

"Yeah, good point. *Wink wink.*" She pauses. "There, that better?"

"Ma'am, if you're flirting with me, your attentions have gone unnoticed."

More chewing. "Because of the dark?"

"Totally because of the dark."

"Well, I'm a horrible flirt, so the dark hardly signifies. But thanks for saying so. I could use the confidence boost."

"I think you're doing okay so far." I hear the sound of her wiping her hands off on something—I doubt it's her skirt, and wonder if she has a napkin or something.

"Just *okay*? That's because I'm not flirting. I can't even see you."

"So? You can flirt with someone you've never met, trust me."

"Are you talking about online dating?" She sounds skeptical.

"Yup. Or messaging someone."

It sounds like she's leaning closer, her whisper coming out of the dark. "I'll tell you a little secret, if you swear not to tell anyone."

I shiver despite the stuffiness inside the elevator car.

I nod. "Deal."

"Okay. But remember, we're in this together, because we've been stranded together. No man left behind, got it."

No man left behind. *Now where have I heard those words before?*

"I'm meeting someone tonight that I…met on the IOM." She exclaims in a rush, clamping her lips shut.

Drawing back, my back hits the cold wall of the small room. "I'll tell you a little secret, if you swear not to tell anyone." I repeat the words back to her.

"I'm nodding in agreement," She teases. "Spill."

"So am I."

"You're nodding in agreement, too?"

I laugh. "No, I'm meeting someone tonight that I met on the IOM."

Silence.

It stretches on. And on.

"Hello?" Did she pass out? Fall asleep?

"I'm here," she says out of the dark.

"Okay, well—"

"—What's your IOM username?"

Ahhhh…now it's making sense. She thinks I'm the person she's going down to meet. "MentorTeam2—"

"—259." She finishes for me. I think she leans back now, too. I hear her back hit the wall next to me. "*Hi.*"

"McGinnis983?"

Yes, I realize I'm slow to the uptake, but I'm a guy. I can't help it.

"Yes."

"Well shit. What are the odds."

"*Horrible* odds. And yet…here we are."

I want to ask her name, but don't want to spoil the moment. Despite being hungry and stranded in a dark, musty, and old-as-hell elevator car, I'm actually having fun.

"Now I really wish I hadn't been on my phone when you got in," I blurt out. "I saw the bottom of your dress. I'd love to see the top." Jesus, that sounded perverted. "Shit, that's not what I meant."

"Maybe next time you'll pay more attention. And anyway, if we had met by the tree tonight, what would we have actually done? Stood there awkwardly and made small talk?"

I'm terrible at small talk. Business? Yes. Contracts? Yes. Multi million dollar negotiations? Yes.

Small talk? No.

"I don't know about that. I'd have bought you at least a few drinks, though."

"The drinks are free!" A giggles escapes her. "There's a band downstairs. We could have danced?"

Mmmm, doubtful. I don't dance; at least, not on purpose. "Maybe. Or…we could have gone somewhere quiet to talk."

"We *are* somewhere quiet to talk."

"True."

"And we're alone."

"*True.*"

"What if I'm a troll?"

Trust me, I want to say. I've thought of that, over and over since asking you to meet me downstairs. "You're not."

"How do you know?"

I inhale. "I caught a glimpse of your legs."

"My *legs*?"

"Yup. They're showstoppers."

"Wow. That's…thank you." Her voice is breathless and bashful.

I can't help laughing. "Are you blushing?"

"Yes."

"Okay, I have a question for you."

"Go."

"What made you ask me to meet you tonight. Knowing it was against company policy and breaking the confidentiality agreement?"

Good question. I consider my answer before responding. "Well...despite the fact that we'd already broken numerous policies, I don't know. I was curious and—we'd been messaging each other for awhile now, and every time you have a question it turns into a conversation."

"Mmmhmm." She hums.

"Besides. I...well. I don't have the best luck with women. It's easier when it's not face-to-face."

"What do you mean?"

"I mean—for a few months, there was someone in the office I started thinking about a lot, but never quite got up the nerve to talk to, and recently I saw her with someone else, so...Anyway. I can negotiate the shit out of player's salary, but when it comes to women? Women I'm actually interested in? Let's just say I don't do well on the approach."

"Want to practice on me, now? What would you say if this woman was sitting in front of you?"

"I don't—I don't know. *Hi?*" I swear, if she laughs at me...

She laughs. "How about, "Lovely evening for a party, isn't it?"

"Yeah, that would work. Then what if I said, "You look especially lovely this evening.""

"Well, you could say that, but now you're just repeating yourself. Lovely and evening? Er. You can do better."

"How about, "You know, I've been watching you for a while now...""

"No!" Her voice rings out of the dark, all laughter and hilarity. "God no, you can't say that. It's creepy." Then, "Shit. You're not a stalker, are you?"

"No!" Now it's my damn turn to sound indignant. "No, but I can see everything from my office, so it's easy to see what everyone's doing. Including her." Crap. The last thing I want is for McGinnis983 to think I'm pining over some office girl—Meg—when in fact, I'm warming to the idea of getting to know *her*.

"Okay, you get one more chance. Sweep me off my feet. I mean—not me. Her. Us. I mean. I'll stop talking now..."

I clear my throat. "Uh, hey. Hi. Can I buy you a drink or something? You look...amazing tonight, and I know this might seem random, but I've actually been thinking about coming over here for a while now but needed something to drink first. So sorry this took so long."

"I was *wondering* when you'd come over."

"You were?"

"*Yes.*" Is it just me, or does she sound wistful?

I move my hand then, it makes its way across the hard floor. Slides across the ground until it finds her fingers.

I touch them, hoping she won't pull away.

She doesn't.

Instead, her fingers cover mine, and then they're intertwined.

"I know you don't know me from Adam," inside, I chuckle at the cleverness of my own joke. "But can I kiss you?"

"Please tell me you want to kiss me and that we aren't practicing."

"I want to kiss *you*. If you want to pretend, you can pretend there's mistletoe hanging above us."

"Kissmas Eve," she sighs.

"Kissmas Eve?"

"Yeah—that's what I call it when I hang decorations in my condo; the night I put up the *mistletoe*." I hear her grinning as she recalls the details. "I usually have a party with a bunch of friends —I kind of go overboard when it comes to the holidays, and Christmas is my favorite. So I love to celebrate."

"That's...kind of cute." Then I scoot closer, until our hips are pressed together. Twist my torso until I'm facing her in the dark. Run my hand up her arm, gliding it up the soft cotton of her dress. Her skin is warm, the fabric smooth as silk. When both my hands are cupping her neck, I lean in, settling my mouth on hers.

I don't have to search to find it—its like our lips just *knew*.

CHAPTER 5

"You can take my heart. Just don't take my stapler."
MEG

Our lips touch.

Once. Twice.

Tentative at first, until my lips part. Then his mouth is covering mine and we're kissing—kissing like mad in the dark, only the sounds of our heavy breathing filling the otherwise silence.

It's incredible.

My heart beats, wildly, and every cliché I've ever read about wiz through my mind: girl who loves Christmas but is unlucky in love? Check. Girl who longs for the office hottie, but can't get lucky in the end? Check. The 'stuck in the elevator' plot. Check.

"When we get out of here, I'm going to take you on a date," MentorTeam259 says in between kisses.

"What if I'm too old for you? For all you know, I'm Kenneth Hobbs sixty-year-old secretary."

"Then Gloria, I hope you like steak, because that's what we're eating when I take you out."

He kisses the laugh off my mouth with a groan, his fingers finding their way into my long hair. "Please tell me your name's not Gloria."

"My name's not Gloria," I mutter. Moan.

"Thank god." He goes in for another deep kiss.

Then.

Suddenly, like in the movie, the lights flicker.

Flicker, dim, then come on blazingly bright, just like you knew they would.

I feel myself blink out the blinding light, trying to focus on the face in front of me. The large hands caressing my skin.

I know that face.

I am half in love with that face.

"Adam?" His name is a barely audible gasp.

His eyes are wide with shock, hands still in my hair.

"*Megan?*"

This entire time, I've been sitting on the floor, in the pitch black elevator car, talking and flirting and laughing and with *Adam* Roberts. Adam. Roberts. The guy I spend half my professional career staring at longingly but haven't actually talked to.

He grin is less than shy. "I didn't know you knew my name."

How is that possible? "How could I *not*? You're directly across the hall from me."

My heart takes an extra beat. "I didn't know you knew *my* name."

"How could I not? You wear the most festive outfits of anyone I've ever met."

I feel my own face fall. Of *course* that's how he associates me— that's how everyone in this office knows me. He's probably made his own bets on what I'm wearing tomorrow. I wonder briefly if he's won any money, but when I feel a stab of disappointment run through me, I push the thoughts away.

"You look really beautiful tonight."

I glance up at him.

I wasn't expecting *that*.

"Thank you. So do you. Very handsome."

He chuckles, leaning in to kiss the tip of my nose. "Thanks."

Adam looks around the elevator briefly. "I wonder if the lights coming back on means we're going to start moving soon."

I kind of hope we don't. Now that I know it's Adam, I kind of hope we stay dangling in midair, defying a plummeting death, all in the name of clandestiney, should the hydraulics go the same way as the electrical has. To shit.

Ok, I change my mind. I don't hope we stay trapped in this deathtrap.

But I do hope Adam wants to hang out for a while longer. Kiss me more.

Somewhere safer.

"How long do you think we've been stuck?" I ask as we stand up, since I don't have a watch or my phone handy.

He looks at his wrist to check the time. "About an hour. Not too late to hit the party; now I can buy you that drink."

Adam finally drops his hands, my eyes land on them, searching for a wedding band. I don't find one, but my stomach still plummets. "Wait. No. We can't. You're…married, right?"

Oh god, I'm a home wrecker!

He gives me a quizzical look. "Married? What gave you that impression?"

I snap my mouth shut. Shit. Why did I say anything? Now he's going to think I'm a creepy stalker. Think, Meg, think.

"Um, I saw you at the mall last night buying toys for kids. I just assumed that meant you had a few." *Please tell me I'm wrong, please tell me I'm wrong…*

He smiles. "I was buying a couple gifts for Jason Hart's kids. I don't have any myself—not yet anyways."

My ovaries flutter.

"Or a significant other of *any* kind—I would never cheat one someone I was in a relationship with. Never."

I know what he's thinking; that we see so much of it at work. Athletes and talent cheating on their spouses and needing us to cover it up. Damage control is only part of the game when dealing with high profile celebrity athletes. Trust me, our Public Relations department works around the clock to make some of those guys—who cheat on their spouses regularly—look like saints.

My heart soars.

His hands fall to his sides, and he stuffs them in the pocket of his slacks. The same clothes he wore to work—dammit Sheila!

"Anyway," he's saying. "I could say the same about you."

"What do you mean?" I ask.

"Aren't you seeing someone?" He scratches his chin. "I saw you at the mall last night, too. Getting a picture taken with Santa. Who's your boyfriend?"

I cock an eyebrow at him. "Are you asking if Santa is my boyfriend? Because rest assured, I would have gotten that pony I asked for if he was. And since I don't have that pony…well, you can come up to your own conclusions."

I snicker.

"I wasn't asking about that perv." I frown at him, not quite understanding why he holds such distain for the man in red. "I was talking about the tall dude you left Santa's workshop with.

That guy."

Who on earth is he talking about? What tall dude? There's no one that I…

Ah. Now I know who he's talking about. "Cody? My next door neighbor?"

"Oh." He looks kind of crestfallen. "Well I guess that makes it really convenient."

"What do you mean?"

"Just for dating purposes and stuff." Stuff. What guys says stuff when referring to sex? I mean, that is what he's referring to, isn't it?

"Are you talking about sex? Trust me, I don't have sex—or stuff—with my neighbor." I stare at him for a minute and then burst out laughing. "Cody is my very *gay* next door neighbor. I love him, but we spend our evenings watching chick flicks and painting each other's toes."

He glances down at my feet. "Well Cody did a nice job. I like the red."

"Thank you."

The elevator moves, jolting us both.

And just like in the movies, when I almost fall, Adam catches me. "Gotcha."

* * *

ADAM

SHE'S STANDING at the Christmas tree when I approach, it's blue ornaments bright and shiny amongst the glowing white lights. The white star on top is unlit, like it is every year, but that does nothing to detract from its beauty.

Hey. Maybe I am catching a little holiday spirit, after all.

I clear my throat. "Uh, hey." She smiles at me, amused. "Hi. Can I buy you a drink or something? You look...*amazing* tonight. Incredible, actually—and I know this might seem random, but I've actually been thinking about coming over here for a while now but needed something to drink first. So sorry this took so long."

Her lips twitch. "I was wondering when you'd come over."

"You were?"

"Yes."

I move in closer so my lips are close to her ear, and now I know what she smells like: sugar and spice and everything nice. And sweet. "You really do look beautiful tonight."

"So you do." Her reaches up to brush what I suspect is an invisible piece of lint from my collar. "You're so handsome."

"I know you don't know me from Adam," I say, chuckling. "But can I kiss you?"

We grin at each other.

"Please tell me you want to kiss me and that we aren't practicing."

"I want to kiss *you*. If you want to pretend, you can pretend there's mistletoe hanging above us."

"Kissmas Eve," she sighs.

"Your favorite," I add.

"We are so cheesy." She laughs. "But I love it."

"Right, but do not tell anyone, or so help me God…"

I look up at the unlit star atop the tree; it rests lopsided but sparkling brilliantly. I swear it shines just as brightly as if it were…

It twinkles.

I blink, taking Meg's face in my hands. Kiss her.

Once.

Twice.

Three times.

And on the fourth, we open our mouths just slightly, reaching for each other with our tongues. She tastes of bourbon and Christmas.

"By any chance, were you over by Sheila and the gals from accounting after you stole away to text your friend Tabitha a few minutes ago?"

Her eyes widen. "Yes, how did you know?"

"The bourbon," we say at the say time.

Suddenly, Jason's words come back to me. *"If you don't ask, you'll never know."*

"Never know what?"

Huh. Either she can read my thoughts, or I said that out loud. "Meg," I say pulling back so I can look down at her. Into her gorgeous green eyes. Damn, she's beautiful with her half-lidded gaze. "Do you want to come to a *real* Christmas party with me this week? Not an office party, but a real party with games and food and gifts?"

Her eyes light up. "I would love that!"

"As my *date?*"

"Yes," she says and leans for me again, kissing me again and wrapping her arm around my neck to hold me tighter. "Yes."

"Wait. I forgot one little detail." Shoot, how do I put this. "It's an Ugly Christmas Sweater party."

"Oh!" She waves me off. "No worries. I have an Ugly Christmas sweater. Actually, according to half the people in this room, I have a ton of them." She laughs and leans in for another kiss. "Did you know they place bets about my Kissmas attire?"

"Uh…"

"It's okay. Sheila's not very good about keeping secrets. I'm her winningest *horse.*"

Her winningest horse? What the hell does that mean?

Maybe it's time to have a chat with HR about Sheila's office etiquette.

"One more thing." I push her away, hopefully the final time. "What does this sweater of yours look like? There's a contest and I need yours to be really, really ugly."

"A contest? Nice!" And then she blushes. "Well, I won't lie; it's really ugly. I mean, I know I wear some tacky things this time of year, but you might actually be really embarrassed to be seen with me in this thing. Maybe I better not wear it…"

"It's that bad? That's is fantastic news!"

"Seriously?"

"Yes. You have to wear it—I'll be wearing one, too."

"Alright, alright—you win. But for the record, it's green and stupid fuzzy. It's got the Grinch on it. And it's covered in bells. They jingle and Sheila loathes it with a passion."

I want to say Fuck Sheila, but instead I I throw my head back and laugh. She just described the exact sweater Addison got me last year.

"Why are you laughing?" she asks. "I can get something more toned down if you want?"

"Oh no," I say cupping her face. I plant a kiss on her pink lips. "That sounds perfect."

She smiles at me and we lean in to each other.

"Merry Kissmas, Meg."

"Stop talking."

I stop talking.

Instead, I kiss her.

ACKNOWLEDGMENTS

(TO THE TUNE OF JINGLE BELLS)

Dashing through the snow, she made the cover right…
Alyssa Garcia made it fast, she also made it bright! (*Ho, ho, ho*)
Dashing through this book, we didn't have the time…
We wrote it anyway, with word count on our mind! (*Ho, ho, ho*)
Of all the stress we add, we brainstormed through the night!
Kristin Phillips checked our errors, two author Holy-terrors! (*Ho,
ho, ho*)
Alexandria Bishop shines, we're glad she doesn't sleep!
She formatted this book, it looks so spark-ly sweeettttt.
Our families think we're nuts, most likely cause we are…
The End!

ME Carter: *Dude. That doesn't even go along with the tune!*

Sara Ney: *Yes it does!*

ME Carter: *Uh, no it doesn't. You never actually did the Jingle Bells part.*

Sara Ney: *Wrong song? Dashing through the snow—is that not Jingle Bells?*

ME Carter: *Whatever. Close enough.*

And now… New Year's Steve!

New Year's Steve

USA TODAY BESTSELLING AUTHOR

SARA NEY & M.E. CARTER

NEW YEAR'S STEVE

PART I
THURSDAY

The day before NEW YEARS EVE

FELICITY

"*All* I want for New Years, is youuuuu, bay-bee…"

I am still feeling that post-Christmas buzz.

The eggnog might be dried up from the holiday party, but my desk chair is swiveling, and I'm humming along to the same song I started playing November first. Sure, I might have to change up the words to suit the current holiday fever in the air, but as long as the radio keeps playing it, I'm going to listen.

No one can hear it anyway; last year I was promoted and with that comes a swanky private office.

I kick the volume up a notch on my wireless speaker perched in the corner of my work space and flick the gold, black, and silver streamer the office administrative staff decorated my computer monitor with, fingers and pen tapping along to the tune.

"…I just want you for my own, more than you will ever know…" I sing, voice cracking because I may be a lot of things, but a musical diva is not one of them.

I pause when the overhead light above me flashes, more suited to a Halloween fun house than an office space, and frown. I stop singing to stare, waiting and watching for it to flash again.

Flicker.

There!

There it goes!

This will not do. I cannot be distracted by the damn light flashing and flicking and doing whatever else it's going to do while I'm busting my ass to get these Year End reconciliations done. I simply do not have the time to be distracted.

Despite my *repeated* calls to maintenance over the last two weeks, the guys down in that department haven't found time to fit me in. Which means I've been living with the occasional blinding light for fourteen days.

This feels oddly like I'm back in college, living in a crappy house with a group of my friends, trying to get the landlord to come fix something that we wrecked. A broken smoke detector. The handle falling off the front door. *Catch the bat that got in through the chimney...*

Still, I shouldn't have to wait two entire weeks for someone to come take a look at this! Bring a new lightbulb, fix a wire. I don't know — something to make it stop!

My eyes stray to the cubicles outside my office and the hustle and bustle of everyone working for the McGinnis Agency.

Hustle, hustle, hustle.

No one is stopping to chat, everyone wanting to finish early and head home because tomorrow is New Year's Eve.

In spite of the jacked-up lighting, I'm feeling fantastic. I've been in my groove, fingers moving like rapid fire over the keyboard as I work in the accounting software, reviewing those reconciliations to check and double check that all entries can be made prior to close of business tomorrow.

And as a reward for all my hard work?

My date.

It'll be the first time I meet the man I've been chatting with online and on New Year's Eve no less. I'm equally excited and nervous, but mostly stressed by how much needs to get done before then.

The clock is ticking on this deadline, but I'm the department head and know we're going to finish in time. I keep my head bent over my keyboard, glasses perched on the bridge of my nose, working away.

Even if I have to stay all night tonight — alone — and work this late tomorrow, we are going to get these ledgers finished. No rest for the weary and all that jazz. I'm willing to do the work on my own, even though I have an entire team behind me busting their butts, too.

I roll my chair backwards to swipe a sheet of paper from the printer, and the lights flash.

Flicker.

Flicker, flicker.

I frown as there's a soft knock at my door.

"Knock, knock." It's Meg McClaren, one of my work friends who's also one of the best female sports agents in the business.

Meg walks in and perches herself on the end of my desk, poking the tip of her fingers at a glittery little disco ball that will double as my own personal ball dropping tomorrow if I'm not out of here by midnight.

"Tabitha and I are going downtown for lunch, wanna come?"

I sigh because I like them both so much, but groan because I can't go with them. There is just no way. "Ugh, I'd love to but I can't." I lift a sheaf of papers off the desk then set them back down. "I have to enter all this into the system, and I don't want to lose an hour." I frown at her. "I'm sorry."

Adulting is hard.

My friend stands, the black tights she has on sparkle with silver stars, catching the light. When it flickers again, she glances up. "What's wrong with your light?"

"No idea but it's driving me bonkers."

"You should call maintenance," she tells me helpfully.

"I have. Like a dozen times. I don't know what I have to do to get someone up here. I'm going to be cross-eyed pretty soon."

Flicker.

She wrinkles her nose and huffs. "That's bad. How are you getting any work done?"

I shake my head. "Just powering through, that's all we can do."

She walks back to the door, leaning against the frame. "I'll bring you something from your favorite taco truck so you remember to eat."

The look I give her is a grateful one. "Oh my god, I would love you for that."

Her hands give a little tap. "Okay — don't work too hard and I'll be back in a bit."

Right.

Okay, Felicity. Focus.

Minor interruption, big task trying to regroup.

I shake my hands and stretch my fingers, blow out a puff of air and sip from the mug resting near the funky blow up letters that say HAPPY NEW YEAR!

So cute.

Grinning when I bend my head, I do my best not to let my thoughts stray, reciting numbers in my mind. Accounting things. Numbers. Adding. Debits. Credits.

Steve, Steve, Steve.

Stop it, you have work to do. Your date isn't until tomorrow night.

For the briefest of a second, the fluorescent panel above me goes off again.

"You have *got* to be freaking kidding me."

Irritated, I swipe the phone off its cradle — the old-fashioned kind where you have to poke the buttons with your fingers and not tap a screen — and dial the maintenance office for the umpteenth time this week.

I'm not even a bit surprised when Old Man Skeeter (the head of maintenance) doesn't answer and frustrated, slam the phone back down.

"Come on, seriously?!" There has to be someone down there. This building is huge, I'm guessing there's at least a dozen people on the custodial staff.

Leaning back in my chair, I stretch my bunny slipper clad feet out in front of me. Taking a deep breath, I dial the number again, looking up at the ceiling while I wait for the beep I know is coming.

Beep! "Hi Skeeter. It's Felicity in accounting. Again. The florescent light above my desk is still flickering and it's starting to give me a migraine." It's not, but I'm not above using dramatics at this point. "If you can please send someone my way to fix it, I'd be so grateful. There's no better way to start off the New Year than with a new light, right?"

The fuck?

A new light? How about sending me one that works!

I frown at my own stupid use of words, seriously needing to focus my attention on these numbers so I'm not stuck here until tomorrow night. Cancelling my date would royally suck.

It's either that or doing something drastic like "accidentally" photocopying my butt as the ultimate procrastination.

I realize that I'm still holding the phone.

Shit. "Okay, so thank you."

I quickly hang up, reaching for my favorite mug with the Winter Camellia printed on it, and decide I need a refill. Heading to the break room to get more chocolate milk is just what I need to get my head back in the game. And yes — I am a grown ass woman drinking chocolate milk out of a flower mug. What can I say? It's not a crime, it's my guilty pleasure.

Throw in some ice and it tastes like a milk shake, la di da!

I'm so fancy.

Cell in the palm of my hand (because it goes with me everywhere, let's be honest), I head upstairs one floor where the good break room is. Just as I exit the elevator, my heart skips a beat when I see a LoveSwept message from Steve.

Steve: *Haven't heard from you in awhile. Just wanted to pop on and tell you how excited I am for tomorrow night!*

For weeks, he and I have been flirting over an online dating app. He seems kind and smart and genuine. I love the mysterious vibe he has, along with the faceless pics he uses. His looks remain to be seen, because he's that guy online with silhouette pictures or, worse, a blurry face, but I will say this: his profile boasts a strong nose and chiseled jawline.

Gainfully employed. Athletic. Loves to travel and is looking for his partner in crime.

Hellooo, he's a keeper, I just know it. And did I mention, his witty banter is on. point.

Better still, he's asked me if I'd be his New Year's Eve date! New Year's Eve with Steve.

New Year's Steve.

"Ha! That's funny. Good one Felicity."

Oh man, I need to get out more. My jokes suck.

But I can't go anywhere until I have to get these last accounts reviewed, and the light keeps making my eyes bug out, so it would appear that I'm at something of an impasse.

Which means, I have to take matters into my own hands, and handle the lighting situation in my office myself. And by myself, I mean I'm going to go hunt someone down, not fix the actual problem. Once I get my chocolate fix, of course.

MY PHONE SCREEN ILLUMINATES AGAIN, Steve's name popping up and making my heart sore.

Steve: *Less than 24 hours!*

Ugh, he is so romantic!

Mug in hand, I hang a right toward the break room,

wandering through the lobby, heading toward the bank of elevators on this floor.

New Year's decorations are on full display out here, too, spreading that McGinnis holiday cheer.

The McGinnis Agency may be known for representing some of the best and biggest sports names in the *world* and raking in millions upon millions of dollars in commission rates per year, but if the company goes belly up? They can always move into holiday party planning.

No expense is spared on a McGinnis Office party. Even the elevators are decorated. Pretty sure someone even put up some mistletoe in there until HR made them take it down (and I'm pretty sure it was Meg).

Funny how Skeeter down in maintenance jumped right on *that*. I saw the crotchety old goat tearing it down with a grin on his face.

New Year's Eve falls on a Friday this year, which means we'll all still be working. Maybe not a full work day, but the staff is supposed to be here just the same. Sports agents never get a day off; not when their clients are playing in championships, Pro-Bowls, tournaments, play-offs, games — you name it — on any given holiday.

I may just be an accountant, but I put in the hours, too.

Me: *Hey, I was just thinking about you. I'm excited too! And technically it's eighteen hours, thirty-two minutes — but who's counting LOL.*

Just as I'm about to slide my cell into the tiny pocket of my pencil skirt, my phone pings again.

"Eeek!" I squeal that his reply only takes a few moments — something I love about him — marveling at the fact that Steve isn't the type of guy who waits to text back purposely to play it cool.

My bunny slippers shuffle along the tile floor as I make my way to the break room fridge.

Yes, I'm wearing bunny slippers with my business attire with no shame. At least I have a skirt on. You never know when someone important is going to request a Zoom meeting, and you find out the hard way your camera angle is set wrong.

I've never been caught in a precarious position like that, mostly because my co-worker Frank learned *that* lesson for us all.

Twice.

I really shouldn't know he's a Fruit of the Loom *whitey-tighty kind of man.*

I swipe right and open Steve's newest message.

Steve: *Good thing one of us is good with numbers.*

I take a quick moment to do a happy dance, then blow out a calming breath and type.

Me: *It's not the nerdiest thing about me, you know. I was on the chess team in fifth grade, so there.*

Steve: *Oh yeah? I had braces in college.*

Braces in college?

That makes me laugh.

Me: *Aww, I bet you were adorable.*

Steve: *Yeah, NO. Literally not a single person thought it was adorable, and by person, I mean girls.*

Me: *Lucky for me I guess.*

See? I can be flirty when I want to be.

Steve: *What are you up to right now?*

Me: *Eh, just some boring work stuff. Need to get it all done so we can finally meet face to face tomorrow.*

Steve: *Are you nervous at all?*

Actually…

Yes.

YES. I am nervous!

I want to text him "MY GOD YES!" but know that's probably not the best idea. Makes me sound eager and spastic. No need to scare the poor guy away — let him get used to me first before he finds out what an utter goofball I am. No, it's best to play this aloof.

Me: *I feel like it's been a long time coming. Fingers crossed we enjoy each other in person as much as we do online.*

There is nothing worse than two weeks' worth of build up for one giant evening of a letdown. Believe me, I know. This will be my third match in the past two months, and no matter what my gut is telling me about this one, there's always a chance it's going to flop.

Me: *Fingers crossed for chemistry!*

"Honest, yet not too desperate, wouldn't you agree," I say down to my bunny slippers who wiggle in agreement.

My phone dings again, but I force myself to pour my glass of milk first. I have a good feeling about this guy, but there's always that one percent who wonders if it's actually a catfish on the other end.

Once my mug is full and the milk is secured back in the fridge, I take a look.

Steve: *So how long are you going to be at work today? It's a holiday.*

Me: *You consider New Year's Eve-Eve the holiday?*

Steve: *I consider every holiday the holiday, Hallmark or not.*

Oh my god, Meg would love him. She absolutely cannot get enough of Christmas. Christmas trees, decorating, ugly sweaters, ridiculous earrings shaped like ornaments, lights, tinsel…

The list goes on and on and she would adore Steve.

Me: *Which one is your favorite?*

Steve: *Definitely Christmas and Valentine's Day. Haven't celebrated that one in years though, but my dad used to break out all the stops for Mom and that what's I'm looking for too.*

Swoon!

Clutching my phone to my heart, I feel my knees go weak. If Steve is half as sweet in person as he is online, I won't care what he looks like.

The upcoming year *is* looking bright. As long as Skeeter or one of the custodians gets to that light before it dims completely. Or bugs my eyes out and causes me to go blind.

Which could happen. I've seen the documentary.

My stomach growls and I take another chug from my mug, hoping the chocolate milk will coat my stomach until Tabitha and Meg come back to feed me, but maybe I should steal a snack from the cabinet and take it back to my desk — just in case.

I nab an almond bar and a banana, and couple packages of peanut butter crackers because they go great with my milk.

Bumping into Sheila, one of the long-time receptionists on my way out of the break room, I almost drop half my treats. It's worth it when I catch sight of her snazzy outfit.

"Well, don't you look festive."

Sheila twirls, gold tasseled skirt flaring around her ankles, black tights thick and warm to combat the cold outside. Winter boots don't add to the look, but make me smile so in my book that's a win.

I hide it by sipping from my mug.

"Going somewhere later?" I ask her, settling in for a quick chat. The diversion is welcome since I have to go hunt down the maintenance staff, and besides — maybe she can point me in the right direction.

Sheila knows everything.

She nods. "I met someone on Christian Singles. Dwight and I are going to a jazz bar after I'm done cracking skulls."

Did I mention she thinks she runs this place?

"Oh, online dating?" My brows go up. "Me too, how's it working out for you so far?"

I peg her to be about sixty-two or three years old. Snarky enough to be my grandmother and sassy enough to cause a bit of mischief within the office.

Sheila shrugs. "Eh, some of them only want to bone. It's hard to know, just gotta ask."

The milk in my mouth almost comes spitting back out at her

mention of the word 'bone,' and I die a little inside, wishing I was as unfiltered as her.

Bone.

I shake my head. "Is that your polite way of saying older gentleman just want to have sex?"

She tilts her head. "You have no idea how many unsolicited wiener pics I get."

From old men? Ew!

"Should I be insulted that I hardly get any?"

She fluffs her frizzy mane, long jingle bell earrings jingling. "No one wants to see a wrinkled wiener caused by the little blue pill."

I try not to grimace as I blink back the visual images running through my brain. "I don't even know what to say about that."

Sheila looks me up and down. "You can't tell me you're not having any luck."

I smile, conjuring up Steve's broad chest and well chiseled chin and what I imagine the rest of his face to look like, considering I've only seen half of it. Ha!

"It's going… slowly but surely, but you know what they say. Slow and steady wins the race."

"That's what losers say," Sheila informs me. "You have to get out there and date, date, date. It's a numbers game at this point. The odds are better the more men you meet."

"Maybe." I shift my stance. "But I think I'm about to get lucky —I might have met someone. We'll see. We have a date tomorrow night."

"A date on New Year's Eve? What kind of a fellow takes a woman out on the most romantic evening of the year?"

My eagerness deflates a little. "I don't know? I'm hoping it's someone who's genuinely interested? We have tons in common…"

"What's this young man's name?"

"Steve."

Sheila thinks for a second. "You have a date on New Year's Eve with a guy named Steve?"

I nod, grinning. Who knew Sheila and I had a stellar sense of humor in common?

"New Year's Steve." She cackles, earrings making that ting ting jingling noise. "Get it?"

Sheila is laughing so hard now, a single tear forms in the corner of her eye and makes its way down her cheek before she swipes it away with the tip of her finger.

"Oh girly, I haven't had a laugh like that all day — and I saw Frank in his under britches on the last Zoom call."

Now I'm grinning too, and both of us are laughing, and I pray to God I don't continue to call him New Year's Steve in my head. Knowing me, I'll accidentally say it out loud.

A snort comes out of my nose.

"Better not be doing that on your date tomorrow," Sheila wisely intones, now sage with dating wisdom. "Men folk don't like a lady who sounds like a pig. Not unless they like bacon."

"Thanks. I'll keep that in mind." I suddenly remember that I'm on a mission and hit her up for direction. "Hey Sheila, would you happen to know where the maintenance office is? I'm having an issue with my lights and no one is returning my calls."

She makes a 'hmm,' sound. "Office manager hasn't helped you with that?"

Er… Do I mention that I bypassed the office manager after the first request because I thought it would be quicker to do myself?

No. No I don't.

"Uh, I did once. Was I supposed to just drop the subject?"

The receptionist levels me with a stare. "Sweetie, don't try to be a hero. Let the office manager do her job."

Okay, but she's not doing her job, otherwise my light would be fixed. I am woman hear me roar and all that jazz.

"I know, I know. And I would if I wasn't on such a time

crunch. I only have until the end of tomorrow to meet this deadline and the lights in my office are tripping me out."

Sheila gives her head a little shake. "Your timing is horrible. I could be wrong but I'm almost positive the maintenance staff isn't working this week."

I sigh. "But you at least know where Skeeter's desk is in the building, right?"

"First floor, suite 102."

"Thanks. I'm going to jog down there and see if he's around."

She tips her head, puzzled. "Why would you jog when you can take the elevator, dear?"

"I was being..." I wave a hand. "Never mind. You're right, I'll take the elevator."

Better to just agree than to argue over it.

"Don't get those bunny ears caught in the door," she hollers after me as a race away.

"I won't, thanks!" I yell over my shoulder, mug, granola bar and banana in hand in search of Skeeter and the gang. Punching the elevator button with gusto, I'm confident that I'll find at least one person who can help me.

HARRISON

*S*he thinks my name is Steve.

Harrison Steven McGinnis, in actuality, but I wasn't about to put that in my dating bio.

Way too searchable, way too rare, way too easily recognizable.

In my defense, Steven *is* my middle name, and because the whole online dating thing creeps me out, I used it to create a bit more anonymity to go along with my cropped face photos and torso shots.

Lame, I know, but there are way too many shady people out there, woman included. Once they find out what I do for a living, they all start creeping out of the shadows. Hence the fake name.

Felicity.

Her name sounds like a ray of sunshine; something I need in my life. Not that my life is terrible, it's just that I can get lonely like everyone else and dating sucks.

Admittedly, I haven't done tons of it, because let's face it — I don't exactly have the time to meet new women every weekend. Nor do I have any intention of sleeping with random strangers just to get my jollies off. Not worth the headache and the chance I'll wind up banging a Stage Five Clinger I can't get rid of once she's been to my condo in the sky, or seen my expensive car, or had a taste of the good life I can provide.

I'm in search of something meaningful, not a gold digger. Unfortunately, there are plenty of those around. I've known that type almost all my life.

My grandfather Len McGinnis founded this company when I was a boy; a sports enthusiast, his best buddy played for the Mets back when players were cheap and baseball was America's favorite pastime. All Grandpa's friend wanted to do was play ball. Mostly uneducated, he'd played in a farm league and had a tough time signing and understanding the players contract. Luckily, Grandpa could, and helped him work through it and…

The rest is history.

I'm not about to squander a legacy for some woman who just wants a meal ticket; these days, it feels like that's all they're here for.

My phone pings and I swivel in my desk chair — twenty-eight floors above the city — with a smile on my face, that familiar buzz that could only be associated with LoveSwept.

Felicity: *Is it ever acceptable to double dip a chip at a party?*

I laugh.

She's so adorable with these goofy questions.

Me: *Only if you break it in half.*

Was that a dumb answer? What the fuck do I know, I double dip all the time. I have no manners, despite the silver spoon that some may think is in my mouth.

Felicity: *What kind of chip and dip are we talking about here? What's your favorite?*

Me: *Why, are you going to feed them to me tomorrow night?*

Felicity: *You flirt! LOL. It would be so weird if I showed up with food…*

Me: *Au contraire, showing up with food is NEVER a bad idea. Always good. Never bad. Good.*

Felicity: *So what's your flavor?*

It's as if she knows the way straight to my heart — with food.

Me: *Shit, that's a tough one. I'd say tortilla and salsa, but that's too predictable. Eh, maybe queso?? I also wouldn't kick a good taco dip out of bed...*

Felicity: *I would kick you out of bed if you showed up with chips.*

And here we go with the rapid fire questions. It's one of our favorite ways to communicate. Quick, simple, to the point, and lots of fun when you're avoiding the regular demands of the day. It's like speed dating with one person. So far, it's always confirmed we have lots in common, and just enough differences to make things interesting.

Me: *What about crackers when I'm sick? Can I eat those in bed?*

Felicity: *How sick are we talking about?*

Me: *The flu*

Felicity: *Would you settle for crackers on the couch instead?*

Me: *Possibly. Are you rubbing my feet?*

Felicity: *Possibly. Are you wearing socks?*

Me: *Possibly. Did you get them for me as a treat to make me feel better?*

Felicity: *LOL yeah, furry pink ones...*

Me: *I don't mind wearing the color pink. It flatters my complexion.*

Felicity: *Same, LOL*

Pink. Nude.

Whatever works.

Me: *How do you feel about men wearing socks with flip flops?*

Felicity: *Um... Are we talking about OLD men? Cause that's acceptable. If we're talking about YOU, then I guess I'd have to see it before I decided.*

Me: *I could add the photo to my bio so you can see it.*

Felicity: ***eye roll***

Me: *Yeah, you're right. I've never done that.*

Me: *Yes I have.*

Felicity: *LOL you're funny today.*

Me: *It's been a slow day so I'm feeling pretty good heading into the weekend. Tomorrow I'm taking a rare day off.*

Felicity: *What are you going to do?*

Me: *Haircut, jog in the park, grab lunch with one of my buddies. Then, I don't know — I have a hot date at midnight. Wouldn't it be cool if it were at the top of the Empire State Building?*

Felicity: *Like that one movie from twenty years ago? That WOULD be so fantastic... wind whipping my hair in my face, getting stuck to my lipstick. Shouting at each other because we can't hear a thing the other person is saying. SO romantic.*

Me: *OOKayyy so a little too high up for you?*

Felicity: *Maybe. LOL the building I'm in would be more my speed, only thirty floors. Wink wink.*

Me: *Thirty sounds about right.*

Felicity: *Do-able.*

Felicity: *Ugh, I hate to cut this short but I'm on a mission to get some things fixed in my office before I can get back to work. Wish me luck, I have a man to go hunt down.*

Me: *Another man?!*

Felicity: *Now, now... don't be jealous. I'm a one woman man.*

A one woman man.

That makes me smile.

For a long time.

I'm still smiling like a friggin' moron when Sheila sticks her head in my door, frown on her face, long gold earrings jingling.

Sheila was a hire of my father's, who had my position before retiring and leaving the agency's empire to me, and I'll be honest: sometimes she scares the shit out of me.

She is the one person in this place who doesn't put up with bullshit — and believe me, when you have a company built around the egos of some of the world's best and biggest athletes, egos are served up on sterling silver platters with a hefty signing bonus.

Sheila could give a shit.

She doesn't care how much someone's contract is worth, where they're from, where they're going, or what they're wearing — she treats everyone the same.

The woman really gets around.

Technically she's supposed to be on the floor below me, but there is nothing she loves better than to float. And by float, I mean walk around gossiping and interrupting everyone while they work. What does she actually do here again?

It doesn't really surprise me considering we're from an entirely different generation. My dad used to do the same thing. He called it "boosting team morale." I called it leaving the actual work to me. I ended up with his job so I guess I can't complain.

"Hey Sheila, what's up?"

"A few of the gals were wondering if you wanted the New Year's decorations taken down before the weekend, or on Monday when we get back."

"And by 'few of the gals,' do you mean you?"

She's a stickler, this one. Nothing gets past her and disapproval from Sheila — the real boss — means the fun is over.

"No, smart ass, Donna."

Literally the only person here with the balls to call me smart ass to my face. I squint at her. "Remind me again who Donna is?"

"She's the assistant to your office manager, Beth."

"Oh." I rack my brain for an inkling of an idea who she's talking about. Donna must be new. I can't keep up with all the new hires these days. I give up and shrug. "I guess it doesn't matter when the decorations come down. Maybe it would be easier if they were left up until Monday. Let everyone enjoy them tomorrow."

Sheila nods her approval. "That's what I told her." She leans against the doorframe. "Any plans for the weekend?"

"Are you asking if I have anything going on for New Year's Eve?"

Nosey.

I lean in my desk chair, letting the springs creek until it's almost all the way tipped back, and stretch before responding.

"I have plans with someone, yeah."

No way am I going to tell her what those plans are, or with whom. I don't need every woman in this office to know my personal business. Not to mention, Sheila has a tendency to also gossip with our clients. Like I need Lebron Sutton — Super Bowl MVP two years in a row — gossiping with the receptionist and knowing I haven't been laid in four months.

Which has happened before.

Lebron + Sheila = huge pain in my ass.

She's blinking at me silently, waiting for more detail.

Nope. Sorry.

No.

I barely share this shit with Adam, my best work friend, let alone the sixty-five-year old watchdog who patrols the hallways like she's security. The bars downtown should hire her to throw people out, she's that damn formidable.

I raise my brows.

She raises hers.

It's a battle of wills she will not win. I am not backing down.

Finally, "Are you coming in tomorrow boss?"

My head goes back and forth, wishy-washy. "Probably not. I'm having lunch with Adam. We'll see if he meets me or not."

Sheila nods. "He's still dating that McClaren girl. I wonder how long it will be before they bless us with a McGinnis baby."

Oh boy. *Here we go.*

If there's one thing Sheila loves besides gossip, it's babies. And if there's one thing she loves more than babies, it's pushing me to have one.

"Does this someone you have plans with tomorrow like children?"

Yes. "Don't most people like children?"

Sheila shrugs her bony shoulders. "Not me."

That makes me laugh. Of course she doesn't like kids. Babies, yes. Kids, no.

"So just babies then?"

"Just babies." She pauses. "But only to hold for a few minutes, then I give them back. I am not a nanny."

Right.

I'll remember that.

"Has this person you're going out with tomorrow night been to the office?"

I narrow my eyes. Wow, she is really good at this. "No."

Shit. Did I just give away the fact that it's not someone from work that I'm going out with tomorrow night? Will she put the pieces together and realize it's a first date?

I cough.

Hint, hint, time to go.

My phone buzzes loudly and I use the opportunity to dismiss her by lifting a finger. "Oh, better reply to this."

She is not deterred. "What kind of an odd notification sound is that?"

Um. A dating app sound? "It's my, um. Doctor's office."

She wrinkles her nose. "They're calling you during the holiday?"

Buzz, buzz. "It's technically not a holiday yet, Sheila. I really have to reply to this. If you'll excuse me."

The receptionist eyes me like a hawk a few more seconds from her place at the door before turning her head and strolling away, on to find her next victim.

I exhale, body relaxing.

Sheesh.

PART II
FRIDAY

Aka: New Year's Eve

Welp.

Skeeter was nowhere to be found, and trust me, I looked for him good and long yesterday before heading back to my office to crank out more work.

I finally gave up looking because I was wasting so much time, strolling around in my bunny slippers and cradling my mug of milk. No one would understand the amount of pressure I'm under. They just see a whack job roaming the lobby; all I'm missing is a bathrobe and a few cats trailing behind me.

Although if my date tonight doesn't go well, I might consider going the crazy cat lady route. Steve seems absolutely perfect on paper, er, or online. Whatever. If he turns out to be a dud though, I'll have lost all faith in the dating pool.

That's probably not true. I tend to be a glutton for punishment when it comes to eating out, so eventually I'll get up to try, try again. I'm just so damn excited to finally meet the man who could be "the one". I can't let that one percent of doubt put a damper on my mood.

And I can't let my fantasies squash my productivity. I'm *this close* to finishing these reports and the clock is ticking.

Clasping my fingers out in front of me, I stretch out my back and rock my head back and forth. Deep breaths, Felicity. And go!

Flicker.

You have *got* to be fucking kidding me.

Flicker, flash.

No. I will ignore it. I will pretend it's not taunting me. I will push my glare-reducing glasses back up my nose and finish this report, demon possessed lightbulb be damned.

I quickly blow out a calming breath as I wiggle my fingers and place them back on the keyboard, depressing the space bar.

Flicker, flicker, flicker.

"UGH! Are you serious right now?" Slamming my hands down on my desk, I look up and glare at the offending tiles above as if God is watching and having a laugh at my expense — and sanity. "You're doing it on purpose, aren't you? Waiting until I type to interrupt, huh?"

He doesn't answer so I huff and lean back in my chair, trying to control my rage while recognizing I may need a quick vaca in one of those places overworked celebrities call "spas". Preferably one that provides Xanax and a pillowtop mattress. The strobe like effects above my head shouldn't produce this amount of anger, but there is only so much one woman can take. And I've been taking this for weeks now.

Plus, it's New Year's Eve and I know I'm in for the long haul.

Snatching my office phone off the cradle, I press the keys harder than necessary to dial Skeeter's number. At this point I know it by heart, and doesn't that just piss me off even more. Who in their right mind knows the seven digits to maintenance off the top of their heads? This crazy. That's who.

As it rings, I remind myself to kill Skeeter with kindness, even if at this point I want to just kill him in general. But no. I am a strong, stable woman. I will remain calm and professional in my bunny slippers.

Okay maybe I'll just remain calm.

I stretch out my body and stare absentmindedly at the ceiling, forcing my breathing to remain under control.

Flicker.

I flip my ceiling the bird. "Take that motherfuc…" *Beep!*

"… Skeeter! Felicity again, hiiiii. Listen, I know today is the last day of the year and I'm sure you're busy with end of the year stuff like I am—."

I roll my eyes at myself and my insane ability to blow smoke up someone's ass during the most dramatic of situations. Although, clearly it isn't having the desired effect so I may need to revisit how much cheer I force into my voice at a later time.

"It's been weeks now that my light has been going out and it's making it very hard to concentrate. We're talking hostile working environment here, Skeets."

Skeets? That's a whole new level of smoke.

"So yeah. Please. I'm begging you. I will give you anything you want. My first born or, or… my favorite mug. Okay maybe not the mug but you get my drift. Hell, you can leave the lightbulb on my desk and I'll do it myself. Yeah. Okay. Thank you, bye."

I hang up, not convinced he'll actually show up any time soon, but even if I wanted to back track and get the office manager in on this, she's not here today. Not many people are.

I've worked here for years and not once have the head honchos been here on New Year's Eve. Most of the tails honchos don't show up either. A few of the lower level agents do, mostly because they don't have office issued laptops to work from home like senior members do. I guess it's just them and me today.

I begin slipping off my bunnies and putting on my strappy stilettos when my phone dings. I know who that has to be. My New Year's Steve.

I snort a laugh to myself. That's still funny.

Steve: *Have you left the office yet?*

Me: *You know it's still morning, right?*

Steve: *You know it's a holiday right?*

Me: *All the more reason I need to finish these reports. I'm ready to take a few days off and start the new year right. Speaking of, have you decided where we're going to meet yet?*

Steve: *Yes. But it's still a surprise.*

Me: *We're meeting in less than 12 hours! I need time to prepare!*

Steve: *There's nothing to prepare for. Dress for a night out and wait for me to tell you where to go. I promise it'll be fun.*

Me: *Fun like, "the lotion is in the basket, Hello Clarice," or...?*

Steve: *Lol. No Clarice. I am not a serial killer. And we'll be meeting in a public place. No worries there.*

Me: *Not worried. Just cautious. You are a stranger after all.*

Steve: *Not for much longer, assuming you get those reports done. I have a lunch date with a buddy so I'll let you get back to it. See you tonight.*

Me: *Can't wait to watch your balls drop with you!*

Me: *Your balls!*

Me: *The ball! Not your balls! I'm sure you have more than one. The big ball.*

Me: *Omg I quit. I'm going back into my hidey hole now.*

Steve: *Hidey hole? I'm dying.*

Me: *No, I am. Don't even look at me, I'm hideous.*

Steve: *LOLOLOLOL. Me and my big ball will see you tonight.*

Fucking autocorrect.

Actually, that's not true. Fucking *flickering light* made my brain spaz out and now I'm coming across like a horny minx. I suppose there are worse ways to act on a New Year's Eve date.

Shaking off my embarrassment because I have no time for it, I buckle the strap on my shoe. I wouldn't normally care about my footwear but I need to find my boss, Victoria. I want her to make sure she got my latest data and she doesn't see any glaring discrepancies.

Triple check and all that jazz.

I grab my mug because I might as well make a pit stop for

refreshments since I'm out. Plus, I don't want to get up from that desk again unless absolutely necessary.

I've got eight hours until I need to be out of here or I won't have time for the necessary pre-date gaming. A good self-grooming takes time and while this is a first date, a girl has to be prepared.

"Hey Vic," I call out as I peek my head into her office. "Did you get my…"

I stop mid-sentence.

The lights in her office are dim and her computer is off.

She's not here, dammit!

Honestly, I'm not that surprised. If I had a nickel for every time she was a no-show on days like today, I'd have enough money to have quit long ago. It's not a company holiday but when the big wigs aren't here, half the bosses don't show up either.

I suppose it means she has a lot of trust in my ability to get the job done.

It also means an extra paid vacation day for me when I remind her she owes me for showing up when she didn't. Usually that elicits a glare right before she signs off on my request.

Good enough for me.

My only regret is changing shoes just in case. Poor neglected bunnies. I'll get back to them soon. But first, break room.

I could use the one on this floor, but instead I use the elevator to go up a level. For whatever reason, the agents get the fancy coffee maker and cabinets full of snacks, and right now, I'm in the mood for an upgrade. Us lowly people in accounting get zippo.

I have no idea who buys all the granola bars and fruit snacks, but there aren't any notes saying to keep my mitts off, so I assume they're company issued. If not… well, I can always apologize later.

The ride is short and I beeline for Meg's desk. That's the second reason I like this floor better.

Sneaking up behind her, I get as close as I can before using my full volume to greet her with a "Hey!"

She jumps and squeals, barely missing my face with the back of her head.

"Hey watch it! You could have broken my nose and I don't need to show up with one as an ice breaker conversation for my date. I need to at least try to look like my LoveSwept profile picture tonight."

"It serves you right for sneaking up on me like that." Meg clutches her ugly sweater covered heart. Did she just press a button on her top that makes it sing Aude Lang Syne?

Who am I kidding?

This is Meg — of *course* she did. Not that I have room to judge. I miss my bunnies already. Still, I can't let this moment pass me by.

"Uh… why is your sweater singing?"

Her eyes light up, clearly distracted from her faux heart attack. "Isn't it cute? Adam found it and knew I'd love it. Said it screamed my name."

"Haven't you been dating for like thirty seconds? Is that an appropriate amount of time for White Elephant gift giving?"

"This is not a gag gift. It's the *perfect* gift." She smooths down her top and picks off some imaginary lint. "And gifts are fine. When you know you've found a good one, you just know. Speaking of, shouldn't you be finishing some reports so you can make it to your hot date?"

I lean against her the cubicle wall and sigh. "I'm so close to being done but that damn lightbulb keeps taking my picture. It's driving me up the wall."

"Why don't you have your office manager take care of it?"

"Why does everyone keep saying that? Shouldn't maintenance respond no matter who is calling?"

"Pretty sure the office manager is the one who does or does not approve his vacation days. There's more incentive going that route."

I roll my eyes dramatically. "Fiiiine. When I get back, I'll go through the freaking middle man."

"You are awfully theatrical today."

"That's no different from any other day of the week, today I just have an audience. You."

"Ain't that the truth," Meg says with a giggle and scoots her chair forward like she's ready to get back to work.

That's my cue.

"I'm going to snag some refreshments and get back to it. Don't stay too late today."

"Not planning on it. Once Adam is done with whatever major league crisis he has going on, we'll be heading out until next year."

I lean down and give her a quick hug. "Be safe tonight."

"We will. And let me know how it goes with Mr. Personality."

I stand up straight and clutch my imaginary pearls. "Excuse you. His name is New Year's Steve."

Meg smacks her palm on her face and shakes her head. "Of course it is. Good bye Felicity." She singsongs me away with a wave of her hand and I make a mental note to ask her later about the snowflakes painted on her fingernails.

They're cute. I might need some for my tootsies.

The clickety clack of keyboards greet me as I wind my way through the bank of cubicles. A little further down, there are several offices. Male voices drift out of one of them. I can only assume that's Adam dealing with his crisis.

Seriously, what kind of crisis could a player be having on New Year's Eve? It's got to be a PR issue. As much as I hate that whatever this is could potentially infringe on Meg's evening, it's probably reality show worthy. I should keep an eye on the celebrity gossip news today.

Actually no. No, I should not follow any form of gossip today at all. Otherwise the only date I'm going to have will be in this office sitting at my desk sipping on chocolate milk instead of champagne. And I already know Skeeter would stand me up.

Reinvigorated with motivation, I book it to finish up my task. Holidays wait for no woman, and I'll be damned if I miss this one.

I slow my steps in front of my apartment building, hands on my knees and puffs of air I can see clouding in front of my face. I don't normally jog outside at the end of December, but I needed a change of scenery today. I was hoping for a distraction from my nerves about tonight.

It didn't work.

Now I'm just tired, my toes are frozen, and I keep sniffing because my nose is running from the cold. I should have stuck to the treadmill.

"Did you have a nice run, sir?"

I lift my head to see Fritz, possibly the world's nicest doorman standing next to me. I take one last deep breath before standing up.

"It was cold, that's for sure."

"I can imagine." He pulls the heavy glass door open for me like we've done thousands of times before. "Sounds like it was a great way to end the old year and ring in the new."

"I definitely feel amped up for tonight." I remark as I step into the large entryway to stretch. "What are you doing to celebrate tonight, Fritz?" I like talking to the old guy. He's not the only doorman but he's definitely my favorite.

"Oh, same as every year I suppose. I'll have a quiet dinner and watch the ball drop. Probably the east coast version. I work tomorrow so I don't want to lose any rest."

"So no hot date?"

He chuckles. "Ah my beautiful Imelda's picture will sit right next to me the whole time. That's all the date I need."

Fritz lost his wife to the tragedy of old age a few years ago. And yet he's still one romantic son-of-a-gun.

Clapping his shoulder, I can't help hoping I'm something like him someday. "You're a good man, Fritz."

"You as well sir." He gives me a nod as I head toward the elevator bank and the three thousand square feet I call home.

The open concept space I live in boasts all the upgrades one could hope for in the best school district around. That's not why I chose it, though. I bought this particular apartment because of the floor to ceiling windows. If I lean my forehead against the glass in just the right way and look down, it feels like I'm flying.

It sounds ridiculous but it's nice to feel like I'm soaring above all the problems below sometimes.

Felicity would love it up here.

The view — how it looks at night.

Good god, I've been watching too much Hallmark Channel.

I check the watch on my wrist and note that I only have twenty-minutes to get my ass back up town for my lunch with Adam if I'm going to be on time for my haircut, and while I'm there, I can ask my stylist to shave me.

Kill two birds with one stone...

Hastily, I slide on some fresh deodorant and stumble into the same jeans I had on last night after work, a ball cap covering my sweaty, disheveled mop before heading back to the office.

Not that there's not much for me to do there right now.

That is absolutely untrue. There is *always* something for me to do, but considering it's New Year's Eve, I'm going to let a bunch of shit slide, and most of the executive issues will be on hiatus until the new year begins (which is technically Monday, but who's paying attention).

The biggest issue is waiting for those financial records to be reconciled. Good thing we have a whole team committed to getting it done today. I'm sure they're all hard at work. I should check on that floor while I'm there. They could probably use a private, catered lunch next week.

I text out a quick note to the office manager so I don't forget.

Me: *Hey Beth, for next week — Let's get lunch set up in the conference room for the accounting team. I want to thank them for their hard work this quarter.*

Beth: *Will do! Any special requests?*

Me: *Italian maybe?*

Who doesn't love that?

Me: *Pasta, salad, garlic bread...? Pizza maybe?*

Beth: *That sounds great, Mr. McGinnis. But maybe a bit much for only five people?*

Good point. I keep forgetting the accounting team is small.

Me: *Hold on, give me a minute.*

I put on a beat up pair of sneakers that are too worn to wear running, but just worn in and comfortable enough that I don't have to bend down to tie them.

I push through the fire door on my floor and the stairs to the ground level to continue my workout, shooting Felicity a message as I go. She works in a small office. She probably has an opinion on this kind of thing.

Me: *Quick question. If you were going to bonus a small group of people for going above and beyond, would you do a catered lunch, or... something else.*

Felicity: *That depends. Is this group women or men, or a mix of both?*

Me: *Women.*

Felicity: *Hmm. If it was men, I'd say lunch would be awesome. If it's women and you're trying to show them how much you appreciate them, what about gift cards to someplace nice. Like a spa or something? Who DOESN'T love a back rub?*

Felicity: *Don't get me wrong, lunch is REALLY thoughtful and probably unnecessary.*

Me: *No, you're right. It's only five people and I was just about to order a shit ton of food and figured I'd check with you first.*

I'm standing on the platform between floors ten and eleven, pausing my descent so I can text back and forth without sounding like an autocorrect inept idiot.

Felicity: *Glad I could help!*

I close out the LoveSwept app and shoot off another message to Beth.

Me: *On second thought, what about a few gift cards? What's that spa down on Kilbourn???*

Beth: *Water and Earth?*

Me: *That's the one!*

Beth: *Great choice, boss! I'll get on it.*

Boss.

It's still weird seeing that in writing, or hearing it for that matter. After my grandfather died and my dad retired, the only one left in the family who could run things was me.

Some things about taking over I will never get used to.

I'm at the office in short time — it's not far from my place, but there's no time to walk. And I'm not about to take a cab, so I jog, even though I'm in jeans; do I even care if I get sweaty, since I haven't showered yet?

I'm panting when I make it to the front of McGinnis Head-quarters, stopping to walk off the adrenaline coursing through my veins, pulling my thin winter jacket and tee shirt beneath it away from my body and from under my perspiring armpits.

It's fucking cold out, too.

No doubt I'm going to be a freezing my balls off once my body temperature drops back to normal.

When I look up, Adam is waiting in the lobby, eyes glued to his phone, casually leaning against the desk by the turnstiles looking far more dapper than I am.

Dress pants. Wool pea coat. Red plaid scarf. Black leather gloves.

He puts his hand up when I approach, and we slap each other a high-five.

"Hey man, what took you so long?" He wants to know, stuffing his phone in his coat pocket. "I was texting you?"

"Jogged over."

He looks me up and down. "You look like shit, man."

"Thanks."

We move to the revolving doors and are back in the street, flagging down a cab to head to our lunch reservation.

Well, reservation might be an exaggeration. Adam and I have a standing reservation at a sports bar slash restaurant in the shadier part of town. It's an institution near the baseball stadium, having been around longer than the stadium itself has; dark and dingy, walls covered in memorabilia I've tried to buy off the owner at least a dozen times.

Spence and Boone's.

Except only Boone remains.

Food is fucking fantastic, the locals love hearing the latest insider gossip (when it's not confidential, of course) and Adam and I love hearing the fan's point of view.

Our spot by the window is taken — the place is packed for a college Bowl game — but Boone is working and pulls a table over near one of the flat screen TV's, rearranging chairs and squeezing us onto a table that hadn't existed before our arrival.

It's hella inconvenient, and I feel my cheeks flushing from embarrassment of how much effort is being put in to accommodate us, but who are we to insist we sit somewhere without a good view?

Adam wouldn't let that happen. He loves the special treatment. And when the bills come, we always show our appreciation with a hefty tip. Sometimes tickets to a game, sometimes vouchers for merchandise. Sometimes autographed apparel.

Depends.

Boone has a server bring us our usual draft, whatever IPA is on tap that day from a local brewer, and a basket of chips to occupy us while we wait for our usual lunch: two bratwurst with sauerkraut, mustard, ketchup, and a shared basket of fried cheese curds, and another of fried pickles.

With ranch.

Yeah, yeah, yeah, I know, it's probably going to give me the shits — but we're from the Midwest, give us a break.

"Big plans for tonight?" Adam asks, stuffing a few chips into his mouth, washing it down with the ice water on our table.

"Yes actually — big date tonight."

His eyes go wide. This is news. I haven't had a date in months, and not one I even cared to talk about way back then.

"A date? Like… a first date?"

"Yeah."

"A first date. On New Year's Eve?"

I lean back, tilting my head. "Yeah? Is that bad?"

Adam seems to think so. "New Year's Eve. That's like having a first date on Valentine's Day, man." He lets out a low whistle. "Dude. This is setting the bar way high."

"Maybe I want the bar to be way high. I like this woman."

"Well I hope so, because you could end up with a clinger after this one." He whistles again, chewed chip flying out from between his lips. "Don't get too fancy or you're setting yourself up for a letdown."

"You're being really dramatic."

"Really?" *Chew chew.* "How long have you known this woman?"

"I..." Let's see, how do I put this? "I don't. We connected on a dating app."

Adam pauses before shaking his head. "Dude you are insane."

"Oh that's right, you hate dating apps and dating for that matter — you were just lucky enough to find the love of your life at work, right under your nose."

He scoffs. "That's true — but I didn't know she was right under my nose, remember? We met because she was having technical problems and we accidentally started chatting on the office messenger system."

"And the messenger system is so much different than a dating app?"

He shrugs. "HR already vetted the crazies out for me."

He's got me there.

"Aren't you forgetting about the elevator incident, though?"

He rolls his eyes. "Who could forget about that? No one wants to be trapped inside an elevator at the company Christmas party, especially me. Especially without food."

Maybe. "But if you hadn't, you wouldn't have realized Meg was the love of your life."

That statement he likes. "True. So it stands to reason that maybe — just maybe — there's someone at McGinnis who's your perfect match, you just haven't met her yet."

Right, but it's not the same for him as it is for me. I own and run the company, and you don't shit where you eat, and you don't dip into the company pond. It puts everyone in a compromising position, and I would never abuse the influence I have by making a woman feel obligated to go out with me.

No.

Not going to do it.

There is a no fraternization policy, but the rules are obviously not heavily enforced. It's up to me to hold myself above the regular standard of proper behavior, and lead by example.

"Honestly bro, it's just easier doing it this way. For one, I avoid gold-diggers who only see dollar signs. I don't even want to meet someone at a fundraiser or whatever — they all know who I am before we're introduced. Gold diggers are like piranhas."

Worse actually.

"What's the second thing?" He sucks down some of his beer.

"Secondly, even if it's the daughter of someone wealthy," — say, a team owner's daughter or niece or granddaughter, that's a whole different story — "That's almost worse. Because they only want to date me to maintain their lifestyle — not because they have any interest in me romantically."

He nods because he gets it. "Is there a third thing?"

Yes. "And if I meet someone out in the wild, they see the flash: the thirty-thousand-dollar watch, the expensive car, the silk tie — the smoke." I pop a chip in my mouth, too. "I'm not about that life."

"Uh. The smoke looks more like fart today, man — you look homeless."

That's a stretch. "I do not. My mother gave me this jacket," I press on the down Patagonia, then feel for the zipper, tugging it down and removing it.

"Your *mom* gave you that jacket?" Adam rolls his eyes again. "Wow, if anyone needs a girlfriend, it's you." He laughs. "Your mom. Does she buy your socks and underwear, too?"

I scowl, because yeah, sometimes she does, and who cares? She's bored out of her mind and my dad drives her insane now that he's not working seventy hours a week.

His last idea was to buy an RV and drive it across the United States, but she quickly put the kibosh on that idea.

"So okay, you met this chick where?"

"On a dating app called LoveSwept. That's like, the non-hooking up app for professionals."

"Sure, sure, I've heard of it I think. My cousin just got engaged to someone she met on Sparks, except I'm pretty sure dudes are able to send pictures through that? You know, like dick pics."

"I got what you meant."

No way would I ever do that. The thought of some strange woman taking a screenshot of my nads? No thanks. Besides, men who think their dicks are photogenetic are out of their delusional fucking minds.

"Anyway — New Year's Eve, huh?"

The server chooses that moment to come with our food, placing it in front of us before asking if we need anything else and walking away.

"Yeah — N Y E." I dip one of the fried pickle chips into the ranch dressing, blow on it before popping it in my mouth and scalding my taste buds. SHIT THAT'S HOT. "Except, she doesn't actually know my real name, which isn't that big of a deal, right? But might be weird at the beginning to be like, 'Hey, my name is Harrison, haha.'"

This interests my friend in a big way. "What did you tell her your name is?"

I shrug. "Steve."

"Eh," he says. "I don't blame you. It's way too easy to find people online and shit. You wanna make sure she's normal before you give her all the good details. I get it."

"Exactly. It's not like doing a search for Harrison McGinnis is going to turn up tons of other men. I'm a sitting duck."

"You're a genius." He's biting into his brat, but because we don't have all the time in the world to sit here shooting the breeze, he powers on, even with a mouth full of food. Which is gross, but whatever. "Maybe Meg and I will join you. Where is your date?"

"The hell if I'm telling you!"

"Why?" He pretends to be insulted.

"Because of what you just said — joining us! I do not need an audience when I'm making an ass of myself."

"Just don't wear that outfit tonight, or she's going to think you've spent the day cruising around the block in your Losermobile."

Losermobile?

He's an idiot.

Adam checks his phone, grimaces, sets it down, then wipes his mouth. Chugs half the beer in his glass before announcing, "We have to bounce."

I quickly chug from my beer, too, but stand and reach for my jacket, shrugging it on. Dip into my pocket for my wallet and throw down a hundred-dollar bill.

GRAB MY BRATWURST, because I'm not leaving this baby behind.

"What's going on? Why can't we stay and finish?"

"Manuel Gomez took a hit and they had to take him off the field on a stretcher."

"Fuck!"

Manuel is one of Adam's clients; he's with the Nashville Mountaineers and was in negotiations to sign a more lucrative contract with a three-time Super Bowl winning team.

"That was his mom. They want to see me." He grabs his own brat and slides out the of chair. "I've been fielding calls all day from reporters and sponsors alike, all asking for updates. Vultures. Hell if I know how long he's going to be out yet. Give the doctors a chance to do their work first."

We flag down a cab, of which there are many, and eat our brats on the way, licking our fingers as we head back to the office. From the glare in the rearview mirror, I'd say the driver isn't thrilled about bringing food into his car, but seriously, no way my lunch smells worse than the interior of this thing. Or maybe the smell is just me post jog. Regardless, he'll get a big tip and get over it.

When we get back upstairs, Adam goes his way while I begin to go mine, but not before I tell him, "If there's anything I can do man, let me know."

"I will. Good luck tonight."

We bump fists and I trail along to the bathroom so I can wash my hands after being in the cab; noticing that it's oddly quiet when I make my way to my office.

Strange.

I just assumed more people would be working, considering our clients rarely get a break. Regardless of the time of year, they're too busy entertaining the masses with their physical aptitude to have time off today. I suppose it's primarily just our football clients.

Still.

We represent a good chunk of the active athletes on the field today, and a nice percentage of the retired ones who have endorsement, television, and film deals.

Maybe I should dash downstairs to do a quick wellness check on accounting — it's early enough in the day for them to have time to hit their goal, but the end of the week and the end of the line; just need to make sure they're not buckling under the pressure. Hell, I've got nothing else to do other than check on them. My list is pretty short.

Haircut.

Shave.

Shower.

Date.

Yup, plenty of time to get everything done.

I got this.

I… take a deep breath and realize…

I stink.

Smelling one's own armpits is never the classiest thing to do, especially not out in public, but it's an action I can't stop; not after catching a whiff of myself.

Sweat and fried food.

Ugh.

I stare at my reflection in the gold paneling of the interior of the elevator, groaning at the sight of my stubble, ripped up jeans, worn sneakers, and baseball cap with a shredded brim.

Adam was right. I should be carrying around a cardboard sign right now.

I suddenly regret leaving my jacket on the chair in my office. It sure would have been useful to cover up this mess of a concert tee shirt from the 90s.

I also could have used the sleeve of my jacket to scrub off the grease that's on the inside of the doors when they slide open. I make a note to have Skeeter's crew do a cleaning sweep of the four floors we occupy since the cleaning crew apparently hasn't done it.

Not that I've seen him at all lately. I'll mention it when I see him after he's back from his vacation.

I step off the elevator and look back when it squeaks, the doors sliding slowly closed — then back open, stuck.

Hmm.

Weird.

It wasn't doing that before when I got on; maybe the doors need to be oiled and not just cleaned. Granted, the maintenance guys aren't elevator technicians, but if there's something they can fix before we call in a third party, more power to us.

I push the red STOP button on the inside and the car stays put, halted.

Crouching in front of the power box, I open the small door with the Swiss Army Knife in my back pocket — the one I keep on my keychain — unscrewing it with alacrity.

Peer inside to see if a power switch has been tripped.

I may be no repair man, but I also live in a building with a cargo elevator that routinely breaks down, so I know a thing or two about the basics.

No electrical shorts. No tampering with the control panel.

No...

"Phew! There you are." A cheerful voice is at my back as I stuff the pint-sized tool inside my jeans. "I've never been so relieved to see someone in my life." The voice pauses. "Okay that's overly dramatic — once I was relieved to see Santa Claus in my living room eating cookies, but we both know he's not real and you are."

I pivot on my rubber soles — which squeak the entire way, not unlike the elevator—and stare.

The young woman claps her hands together in mock glee. "I'm *so* glad you're finally here! When you're done with the elevator can you replace that bulb above my desk?"

I have no idea what the hell she's talking about, but she's amusing and I keep my lips shut.

"If you haven't listened to my voice messages, go ahead and delete them — I was starting to sound desperate, ha ha!"

What voice messages?

"I can honestly tell you that I have not listened to any desperate sounding voice messages."

It's not a lie, but it's not an admission that I have no idea who the hell she is. She, on the other hand, apparently knows me? But...

"What do you guys do down there in the custodial office all day? Drink coffee and eat donuts?"

Or maybe she doesn't know me. What is she talking about?

"I'm sorry, I shouldn't have said that — I'm sure you're putting out more fires than I can only imagine. My busted light bulb situation is hardly a priority, not when elevators are breaking and windows have to be replaced."

She looks to me for concession or agreement, and stupefied, I nod.

This girl is…

Cute.

No, scratch that. Not cute — pretty.

And oddly familiar?

Or am I losing my mind because I just had a pint of beer in the middle of the work day?

I find my voice. "I'm sorry, what did you say the problem was?" Sounds like a lightbulb in her office needs to be replaced, and that I can surely do.

After all, this is my office and my responsibility, and how better to lead by example than physically completing a task someone on my team needs help with.

I can lend a hand. I don't have anything to do until four o'clock anyway.

"The light above my desk is flickering and it's driving me insane — I have reports to get done by this afternoon and cannot afford the distractions. You have zero idea how awful it's been! I had to buy a visor to wear to block out the flashing — I feel like a race horse wearing blinders."

She laughs.

My stomach does a strange little roll I recognize as: attraction.

Shit.

Not okay.

1. I have a date tonight with Felicity, whom I've been flirting and chatting with for weeks, and building a foundation with. I know more about her than Adam.

2. This woman works for me, and remember what I said
   earlier about shitting where I eat? Despite there not
   being an enforced fraternization policy?

"I even have a new lightbulb!" She chatters on, leading the way, weaving through a labyrinth of cubicles set up in the center of the main floor. "I know I shouldn't have, but I'm confident that this is an easy fix, and thought maybe I could change it myself? Only that wasn't going to happen because, well — look at me."

Oh, I'm looking at her alright.

Pretty, petite, this woman has curves in all the right places and tiny to boot. I highly doubt she could reach the ceiling unless she had a seven-foot ladder. Even then it's iffy.

"Where'd you get the light bulb?"

"I had it delivered from the hardware store." Her laugh tinkles. "I was going to submit the expense to my boss next week."

Resourceful little thing.

Long dark hair, exotic eyes. Full lips that don't look like they've been cosmetically enhanced.

I know this person.

How do I know this person?

The thought niggles at me until we reach her office; eats away at me like a song playing in my mind I cannot recognize or remember the words to. But I know the melody and the era it's from.

I also know that if I look online, I will find the title and the artist.

Just as I know, that if I look online, I will find this girl.

Call it intuition.

So oddly familiar.

So happy and cheerful.

Her hands are braced on her hips and I realize she's standing in the middle of her office, under a flickering fluorescent light, one of the bulbs going haywire, casting stroke like effects into the room.

"Yeah, that's enough to make a person go blind."

"Exactly!" She's so glad I agree. "Yes, thank you! I'm not going crazy!"

God she's adorable.

How have we never met until now? It's not like I've never been on this floor before. In fact, she's just the department I was coming to see.

"Where is Victoria?" I ask, glancing to the office space next to this one, knowing that is where my head of finance calls home. "I thought y'all were working today to finish the reconciliations."

She doesn't question how I know about the accounting deadlines, or why I'm asking where her direct report is.

"Yes, I thought we were all working today too, but alas, I am a lone wolf. Just me and these."

My ire rises that Victoria has left the heavy lifting to her team, but subsides a bit when I look down to see Cutie Accountant wiggling her toes, feet buried inside the most ridiculous, fluffy bunny slippers.

"Don't tell me you talk to those," I say, stepping into her work space.

"Fine, I won't tell you I talk to them, even though I talk to them," she teases. "Don't judge me, I'm lonely. This is not a glamorous gig."

That makes me laugh.

Accounting may be the least glamourous of all desk jobs but surprisingly, she makes it sexy, probably because of those bunnies on her feet.

"So now what?" she asks. "I'm Felicity by the way."

When she puts out her hand by way of introduction, I freeze, rooted to the spot, unable to respond. At least, not like a normal human person.

My mouth guppies open, jaw hanging slack. "Uh."

Felicity laughs. "And you are…. Tom from Maintenance? Brad? Hank?"

I shake my head, shaking out of my stupor. "Hank? Who names their kid that anymore?" I stick my hand out. "My friends call me Harry."

Zero of my friends call me Harry. Last time they tried, they got punched in the arm, because that was in grade school and I hated that name.

McGinnis. Harrison. Rookie. Shark.

Pick one, those are the options.

Harry makes my ass cheeks pucker, but there you go. I cannot tell her my name is Steve; she'll get suspicious. Tonight was going to be the big reveal — our blind date has to be blind, so I'm going to have to *lie lie lie* and cross my fingers she won't hate me later.

Crap.

Felicity doesn't seem like the kind of woman who will hold a grudge, but I've been wrong about women before so I'll just have to hope and pray.

I like her.

I really fucking like her.

Excitement brews in my belly, the urge to declare myself so fucking irresistible, I want to explode with the news.

"Harry? So, like — Prince Harry from Britain?"

"Zero like Prince Harry from Britain."

Felicity sighs. "But he's so romantic." She tinkles out another giggle. "My girlfriend and I were in London for his wedding, isn't that lame? We flew over and went to a pub in Windsor, and drank Prosecco during the ceremony and chanted and cheered when the crowd went wild."

Yeah, I did know that. She told me when we first matched — it was among her fun, random facts.

I can't remember mine; probably that I can swim two laps in a pool under water holding my breath.

Weak. So, so weak.

"So you're a huge fan?"

Felicity nods. "Mostly of the royal family, more so than anything." She pauses, giving me a side eye. "You think that's weird, don't you?"

I do, but it's not my place to say what someone finds fascinating or not. I collect old coins, and most of my friends thinks that's dumb, so who am I to judge.

"So, uh. I should probably go grab a ladder, right?"

"Oh! Yes, I'm so sorry to be yammering on! Time is money, and here I am wasting your time." She smacks the heel of her palm up to her forehead. "When I start babbling just tell me to stop. I'm hungry but I'm going out to eat later and I haven't wanted to snack so I can eat all the things tonight."

She is so adorable, standing there in her pencil skirt and white blouse with those cute little slippers.

Keeping up this charade may kill me. But if ever there was a time for recon, now is my chance.

FELICITY

*I*t's not weird that the sight of a man hefting a ladder is turning me on, is it?

A man I only just met, with torn jeans and a ratty baseball cap?

That can't be what he wears to work on a regular basis. I'm guessing he's dressed down today since it's a holiday and all, his boss Skeeter is gone and no one is here to reprimand him for the casual attire.

Oh well — suits me just fine.

I follow Harry into the elevator, skeptically eyeing the buttons all the way down, worried it wasn't going to open when we reached the ground floor to get to the maintenance closet because the car is notorious for getting stuck at the most inopportune times.

I can't imagine being trapped in an elevator, on a holiday, with a total stranger.

That is how Meg met Adam.

Actually, they 'met' on the company's in-house messaging system, but had gotten trapped during the company Christmas party on their way down to the lobby, which is as romantic of a story as I have ever heard.

Still. I have no food, no blanket, and no time to get trapped.

I hold my breath the entire trip down, ticking off the floors as we descend, ignoring the hot hunk of a man standing on the other side of the small confined space, fixated on the numbers illuminated above the sliding doors.

Fifteen.

Fourteen.

Ten.

Four.

Lobby.

Ding!

"Were you just holding your breath?" Harry asks as we step out, the relief in me palpable, causing my shoulders to sag in respite.

"Yes. Don't you know how many people have gotten imprisoned in that thing?"

Harry hesitates before answering. "Elevators aren't my area of expertise; I'm assuming the lift company is usually called in to take care of it."

I huff. "They should do a better job. Someone's getting stuck a few times a month. I have anxiety now, and carry granola bars in my bag and a bottle of water just in case."

Plus a little flashlight and back-up battery for my phone.

No joke.

A lady can never be too prepared…

"I'll make a note of that. Maybe give the property owner a call too. Sounds like something more needs to be done than constant maintenance."

Oh… a man who takes charge!

Me like.

I trail after Harry as he heads to the supply closet, doing my best not to glance down at his ass, and it occurs to me that there is zero reason I needed to be accompanying him on this venture.

This is not my job! Why am I not at my desk working? It's not as if I'm going to carry the ladder.

My face flushes with embarrassment, but if he thinks it's strange that I'm following him, he doesn't let on — only hands me the key for the closet and asks me to open it while he bends and takes a drink from the drinking fountain affixed to the wall.

This time I do take a peek at his ass.

But only a quick one! I have a date tonight with someone else.

Bad felicity, bad! You can't date a man employed by your company — you cannot. Hard no.

Plus: there is Steve.

Steve, Steve, Steve.

I push the door to the supply room open and the light automatically goes on, a dingy room filled with gray metal shelving, mop buckets and paper supplies. Brooms, squeegees. CAUTION, WET FLOOR! signs. Window spray and other miscellaneous things, the kind of quick things custodians can come grab in a pinch.

Bet they have another room hidden somewhere else with extra desks, chairs, ceiling tiles, bodies...

At least the last thing I'll see when I die is Harry's handsome face. Or maybe not.

It smells dusty, but there's a ladder.

Perfect.

Harry eases past me to grab it, and I hold the door open for him, then lock up when he's done.

What a team we make. I'm so proud of us even though I've theoretically done nothing and needn't be here.

It's work getting the ladder into the elevator and still have room. It's too tall to stand up straight and barely fits sideways. Harry is forced to hold it the entire ride back up to my floor, but I don't hate the sight of his flexing biceps and strong forearms.

Um. Yeah.

"Thank you so much for doing this — it's going to make a huge difference."

"Not a problem. I had the time."

I nod. "As long as it wasn't an inconvenience."

"None at all." He smiles over at me, teeth straight and pearly, winking at me flirtatiously, and I wish I had something in my hands to occupy them instead of wanting to run them down the front of his soft, cotton tee shirt.

Stop it, Felicity. You are not going to date the maintenance man! You'd want to bang in the broom closet and would never get anything done!

Besides, he's been nothing but professional; even if you were single — which you technically are — a hottie like this isn't going to ask out the woman from accounting.

I imagine he has a date every night of the week.

He's not on any dating apps, that's for sure. I would have seen him, so maybe he's in a relationship. Or married.

I lower my gaze to his left hand; to the fourth finger.

No wedding band. No tan line. No indent.

How convenient.

Maybe he just doesn't wear it, some guys don't. Especially if he's like, sawing things and fixing stuff — wouldn't that get in his way?

That's doctors and nurses and machinists, you moron. They're the ones who can't wear rings.

We make it back to my office and in short time, Harry has the ladder set up beneath my bum light, switch flipped to the off position so he doesn't electrocute himself, and halfway up the rungs he climbs.

When his arms go above his head and the hem of his tee shirt hikes up, bearing a sliver of stomach, I try and turn the other way.

Try to focus on the snow falling outside my window, the frozen pond, the, um.

The… um…

Belly button.

Shit, no!

Not that!

Steve, Steve, Steve.

Harry glances down at me. "Can you take this when I have it unscrewed?"

"Screwed. Got it." Shit. "I mean, yeah — okay."

Oh my god, get your mind out the gutter. You still have tons of work left and a date to get ready for. You do not have time to have flirty thoughts about the maintenance dude.

He hands me the faulty bulb, and I hand him the new up.

Watch as he inserts in, jiggling it to make sure it's secure.

"How does it look?" he asks before stepping down.

"Great," I say, staring at his butt.

He doesn't see me, of course — his eyes are planted on the light, giving it one last test before climbing down and flipping the switch on the wall to power it on.

The room lights up like the Fourth of July, bright and steady.

"Yay!" I clap, unable to stop myself. He has no idea what a relief it is that the lights aren't dancing and short-circuiting, and I can go back to work without the visor shielding my face from the strobes.

"Thank you!"

"No problem." His smile creates a weird flutter inside my chest. "Anything else?"

"Nope, I'm good."

With a tip of the cap, Harry packs up the ladder, and is gone.

* * *

FOR THE FIRST time in weeks, I'm cranking out work with no distractions. It feels good. The reports are compiling, the bunnies are wiggling, and there are no migraine inducing flickers above my head.

Harry is a life saver. I should get his actual number so I can text him directly next time this happens. That would seem too forward, though, wouldn't it? He might think I'm hitting on him when I'm not. There is absolutely no attraction there.

None.

Nope.

Nothing at all.

Okay fine, there is some attraction.

A teensy, weensy bit.

You can't blame a girl for having eyes and Harry is hot in a *blue-collar, not afraid to get his hands dirty, probably the best kind of maniac in the sack* kind of way.

No, Felicity. No.

No, no, no.

I will not begin lusting over Harry. I have a date with Steve tonight.

Steve, Steve, Steve.

But Harry…

Harry, whose low baritone of a voice is what Hallmark movies are made of. With a broad chest and dimple in his chin, and a five o'clock shadow. Deep, easy laugh.

Thinks I'm funny. Didn't care that I was babbling about the British Royal family like a whacko.

Harry, who is tall and funny and smells like a dream. Okay, he smells like cooked meat, but I think he'd probably just had lunch. It's not his fault if onions have an adverse effect on him.

My hormones can overlook it.

Althoughhhh… *Steve* could very well be a catfish or serial killer while *Harry* is obviously real and has been vetted by HR.

STOP, Felicity. Give Steve a chance before jumping ship and jumping Harry.

And before you do either of those things, *finish this report*.

You are here to work, not work on finding a boyfriend!

I push my glasses back up my nose and continue cross-referencing numbers, making quick work as I go. It's amazing what a little distraction free lighting can do for my productivity. Too bad the heaters seemed to have kicked off again.

Leaning over, I put all my brainpower into this report as I pull to get the bottom drawer of my desk open.

I yank. I jiggle it.

I heave.

The damn thing is always stuck!

"Ugh," I grunt as it finally gives way, scowling into it. "Are you in cahoots with the tampon machine in the restroom? I swear it sticks just like this. Isn't that a medical hazard or something? I should probably call Skeeter again."

I grab the blanket I have stored for days like today and wrap the zebra print around my shoulders. My office is the perfect temperature during the summer months, but around this time of year, it's like the heater stops working.

Sufficiently bundled, I take a quick sip of my milk.

"Ahh." Delicious.

Yep. Still ice cold. It's going to be a long winter if this office is such an ice box it keeps beverages cool, but oh well. I got the most pressing issue fixed today. I call that a win.

"Knock knock."

Speaking of winning…

It's Harry, sticking his handsome, smiling face inside my office.

"Hello there stranger."

Oh god. Did I just say that, in a ridiculous flirty voice? Seriously, do I never interact with people or is it only the hot ones I'm attracted to that I struggle with?

Why can't I be hip?

If he notices that I'm awkward, he ignores it and stands there grinning down at me, leaning against the door jam in that way men do when they want to be relaxed and sexy at the same time. All he's missing is a plaid flannel shirt, rolled up to his elbows and a tan from working outside.

But relaxed and sexy? He's definitely both.

"How's the new lightbulb working for you?"

Fantastically. "I will admit, it's a lot easier to get this end of the year reporting done when there isn't a constant flashing reflecting off my screen."

"Good. It's New Year's Eve." The dimple appears in his chin. "I'm sure you have big plans you don't want to miss."

I quirk an eyebrow at him and our gazes lock. Is he… fishing for information about me? Should I tell him I'm unattached and single? Steve doesn't count, we haven't even met, yet.

Still, guilt prickles at my stomach until the truth spills out. "As a matter of fact, I do have plans. All the more reason I appreciate you helping me out. I'm sure you have big plans for the evening as well."

Alright. *Most* of the truth spills out.

Harry nods. "I do. Been looking forward to tonight for a few weeks now."

An odd pang of jealousy hits me out of nowhere. There is no doubt in my mind this super attractive man has a date, probably with someone as equally attractive, because that's what pretty people do. Ugh. Who is he spending tonight with?

Is she beautiful?

Is she his one and only? Are they in *love?*

These are thoughts I shouldn't be having; there's not a single reason to have them. I am going on a date with *Steve*. I'm interested in *Steve*. So why do I feel like there's a weird and strong connection to *Harry?*

"Well, don't let me keep you. I'm sure you need to be on your way, to change and stuff." I give his jeans and scrappy, sweat stained outfit a once over.

Not that I'd toss him out of bed, but the man needs a shower.

Instead of leaving, he cocks his head and studies me in return.

"Why are you bundled up like you're in a snowstorm?"

The question catches me off guard.

For a maintenance man who probably has a list of things to get done before his hot date, he sure is taking an interest in my well-being.

"I don't think the heating unit blows hard enough to reach all the way in here. It gets cold in the winter months." I shiver. "That's how the bunnies ended up here."

I wiggle my feet in his direction and his lips quirk to one side. Pushing off the wall, he makes his way over to my desk and looks up, standing so close to me I can smell him, hands on his hips.

He smells like fried food and musk with a slight tinge of sweat. It's oddly, not an offensive odor. Kind of makes me want to climb him like a tree and see exactly how rough those hands can be.

Down girl. Remember *New Year's Steve?*

But Harry is so nice. And hot. But mostly nice.

And he's here, in my office, whereas Steve... is still just an *idea* of my perfect man.

I sigh. Isn't this always the way it goes. Dating Land is in a severe drought and suddenly it doesn't just rain hot men, it pours.

Just my luck.

Love happens when you least expect it, when you're not looking. I'm pretty sure someone wise once said that to me, or maybe it was a nanna from one of the Lifetime movies they play around Christmas.

Before I can contemplate further, Harry stares at the ceiling tiles making "hmm" sounds in the back of his throat then looking down at me, blue eyes glinting with amusement. I'm not sure what he finds so fun about me freezing to death but there it is .

"I think I may have just solved your heating problem."

This interests me and I perk up.

He points to the vent next to the wall. "See that? Looks like it's closed. All we need to do is turn that spinning nob to open it and you'll be nice and toasty in here."

Did I mention Harry is not only nice, but clearly a genius as well? Where has he been all my life!? Every winter I freeze my ass off in here, and not once has anyone said a word about my damn vent being closed!

I want to face-palm myself back in time to three Sundays from Christmas.

"That's it?" My eyes are probably bugging out. "Just that quick fix to keep my regular shaving from going to waste?"

"Huh?"

His face screws up at the mention of my No Shave November thru January joke, and I'm not about to explain that the hair on my legs adds another layer of warmth.

I wave him off with a forced laugh. "Nothing. Forget I mentioned it. The last thing you probably want is inappropriate visuals about the state of my legs."

I prop one out, extending it and he watches my every move.

Unless I'm reading things wrong, I swear Harry's nostrils just flared with desire. Suddenly I'm glad for the text snafu regarding Steve's balls. Clearly there is an itch I need to scratch if I'm coming across as such a hornball these days.

"Anyway, do you have time to fix the vent before you go?"

"Just need to go grab the ladder again. It won't take but a second."

He turns on his heel and struts out of the office, my head tilting and following the movement of his ass before I can stop myself.

NO!

Guilt hits me once again and I grab my phone for some support, shooting off a rapid fire to the one person who can relate to Inner Office Romance — not that this is what's happening, but it never hurts to flesh out any potential.

Me: *Mayday! Mayday! Harry the Maintenance Man is super hot and I want to lick him!*

Whoa. Coming out of the gate strong, Felicity. Meg is going to think you're a lunatic.

Meg: *Who?*

Me: *I went searching around for Skeeter, from maintenance, and found one of the other guys on his crew to help me and LORD, he's fixing things and smelling male and distracting me and now I'm confused.*

Meg: *I've never heard of Harry. Are you sure that's his name?*

Me: *Positive. Maybe he's new. But who cares? He's super hot and it's making me feel guilt and how would you even know what any of the custodians' names are? How often do you need maintaining?*

Meg: *Fair enough. But I guess...*

Meg: *... I'm not understanding the issue. Some new guy from maintenance is fixing things... and he is better to look at, and smell, than Old Man Skeeter??? I don't see what the problem is here.*

Me: *The PROBLEM is that I have a FIRST date tonight with Steve. Steve! And now I feel guilty for wishing I was free tonight so I could hook up with the super-hot maintenance man.*

Meg: *Sooo... you're complaining that you have two prospects?*

It *is* raining men.

I guess she wouldn't be able to see that as a problem since she's no longer single and ready to mingle as I've been for the past year. She still wants me to play the field, and not settle down, and to wait for "The One".

Me: *(dramatic sigh) Can you just please give me some encouraging words so I can stay on task? Say something like: one man at a time, Felicity. One. Man.*

Meg: *Sorry. Sure.*

Meg: *Although… Realistically you've never met Steve, so he could be catfishing you and really you're going on a date with an 85 year old man named Melvin.*

Me: *That is not helping. You're supposed to be encouraging me to go out with New Year's Steve, the man I've been flirting with for weeks. Not discouraging me.*

Meg: *Oh. Sorry. Let me try again.*

This ought to be good.

Meg: *Harry works in maintenance. There are probably spiders in his hair from all those cobwebs in the basement.*

Me: *I have cobwebs in MY basement (if you catch my drift) so really I can't judge him for that.*

Meg: *You are SO GROSS sometimes!*

Me: *Hey, it's not all sunshine and roses up in accounting, we can't all run around in ugly holiday sweaters and Santa tights and still grab an eligible bachelor.*

Meg: *My sweaters are NOT UGLY. Take that back!!!*

Me: *Sorry, sorry. Let's circle back around and talk about me again. I know that's selfish but I have this date tonight and I'm having all these feelings about Harry…*

Meg: *You are OVERthinking this. Has Harry asked for your number? No. Has he asked you on a date? No. So what you need to do is go out with Steve tonight, have fun, let loose, be carefree. Hopefully he makes you laugh.*

Me: *He makes me laugh in our messages. I think I've really built this up in my head so meeting Harry has thrown me off my game.*

Meg: *Your GAME??? OMG. Stop it right now, you have no game. Your big move is having a man change your light bulb, WHICH BY THE WAY, you could have done yourself.*

Me: *Okay but I didn't have a key to the supply room and even with a ladder I'm kind of short, so technically I couldn't have…*

Meg: *THE POINT IS: Stop overthinking. Have fun. And for the love of god, do NOT forget to report back to me in the morning. I'll keep* *my phone near the bed in case you're doing the walk of shame at dawn and need moral support.*

Me: *I have never — nor will I ever! — do the walk of shame!*

Meg: *Just call me in the morning.*

Meg: *And don't get murdered.*

I roll my eyes, tossing the phone onto my desk with a frown. Overthinking? Yeah, she's right, I probably do that — but I hate admitting when she's right.

I need to focus.

I'm so close to being done I can almost taste the yummy appetizers I'm going to eat tonight at dinner.

So what I need is to get my mind off of Harry — whom I've barely met — and refocus my energy on the man I've been dreaming of meeting for weeks.

Weeks!

We were entering Pen Pal territory — that's an online dating term for when two people message so long without actually planning to go on an actual date, you become Pen Pals. Letters back and forth, no real time interaction. No video chats, no phone calls.

Honestly, I was days away from telling him, "Steve, this has been wonderful but it seems like all you want to do is message back and forth and not meet in person." Then low and behold, he invited me to be his date for New Year's.

Settling back into my chair, I'm pleasantly surprised when I look down at my clock a few minutes later to see that actually, a solid hour has passed and I'm on the verge of finalizing everything.

But what is taking Harry so long to return with that ladder?

As if my thoughts have summoned him, he shows up on cue, carrying the ladder like it weighs next to nothing. Good lord, the sleeve of his shirt is straining his biceps again.

Is there nothing wrong with this man?

Sigh.

"Sorry for taking so long," he says with a smile as he gently places the ladder on the floor and opens it. I push backwards in my chair and I roll out of his way. "I got sidetracked fixing that tampon machine in the ladies' restroom — the one I overheard you complaining about before…"

Oops.

"Turns out someone had stuffed a drink token in it from a casino; guess they were hoping for a big pay-out." He laughs at his corny joke. "Luckily I hadn't returned this to the supply closet." He taps the side of the ladder before climbing it.

And now he's considerate, too? How come a man like Harry isn't on LoveSwept? He's probably one of those obnoxiously awesome people who prefers to build relationships in real life instead of getting sucked into it online. Could he be any more perfect?

Regardless, in no time flat, I feel warm air floating across my desk.

"Holy shit, you did it!" With the way I squeal in delight, you'd think I'd never felt indoor heating before, my hair gently blowing in the new breeze. Ahhh…

Harry quickly replaces the vent cover and climbs down. Snaps his fingers. "Easy fix. Just remember, if it gets too cold in the summer, you'll just need to call and have it closed again. That's what maintenance is there for."

"When I can reach someone," I grumble.

"What was that?"

"Nothing," I say quickly. I don't want to make an issue of how long it took to get this done. No reason for this hottie to take the fall for his boss's failings.

Folding up my blanket, I reach down to pull the drawer open, but it doesn't budge.

Yank. *Tug.*

Grumbling, I yank for a second time, this time the chair and I move more than it does.

I drop my head back on the chair in exasperation, physically spent; I cannot catch a break.

Behind me, a deep, sexy chuckle makes me shiver. "Need me to fix that, too?"

"Would you mind?" I plead, trying to keep the exasperation out of my voice. It's not his fault the entire office building is crumbling around me. Come to think of it, maybe this is why Victoria assigned me this office. It wasn't part of the promotion — it was payback for getting that extra comp day every year.

Sneaky little minx.

"I don't mind at all." Harry's voice makes my lady parts tingle but I quickly rub my arms, playing it off like it's my body readjusting to the warm air.

He glances over my shoulder at the computer monitor when I pull my chair back into position, clucking his tongue. "I'll just return this ladder and grab some WD-40. Looks like you'll have just enough time to cross reference and finish up that last acquisition."

My jaw drops. "You know about acquisitions and reporting?"

He flashes me the sexiest smile I think I have ever seen. Steve better bring his A game on the charm tonight because Harry the Maintenance Man is doing a damn good job of making me forget all about him.

"I know a lot of things about a lot of things."

Oh? Tell me more…

"Then why do you work in maintenance?" I know the question sounds rude, but I'm genuinely curious.

He pauses briefly, measuring his carefully worded answer. "I just like to make sure things are running smoothly around here."

I tilt my head as I absorb his words, but then the alarm on my phone goes off reminding me I have two hours left until I have to be out of here or I will be late. Turning back to my computer, I roll back up to my desk. "Well thank you. I appreciate it so much."

Harry answers with a nod and picks up the ladder effortlessly again. "Truly, it's been my pleasure, Felicity."

The fire in his eyes before he turns and walks out leaves me feeling hot. All. *Over.*

For the first time since I've worked here, I find myself fanning my face to cool down in the winter. And I have Harry to thank for that. In more ways than one.

HARRISON

Things I've learned about Felicity since I matched with her on the LoveSwept dating app:

1. She is looking for something long-term
2. Two older brothers
3. Parents still married
4. Her best friend works at the same company, which I now know is mine, so I wonder who that friend could be.
5. She loves hot dog stands and carnival food.
6. Green eyes. Brown hair. Bright smile.

THINGS I'VE LEARNED about Felicity since she found me at the elevator bank, thinking I was the maintenance man, and hauled me down to her office to fix shit:

1. She's petite and pixie like.
2. She has bunny slippers and a flirtatious laugh.

3. Her voice gets me hard.
4. Her hair looks like satin and I want to run my fingers through it.
5. She keeps pictures on her desk of her trip to London, cat Fiskers, and a small picture of a world map that says, 'Not all who wander are lost.'
6. She smells like strawberries and fresh air.

I'm waxing poetic when I make it back to my office, the office a veritable wasteland by now. It's early afternoon and I'm sorely behind schedule, half the things I needed to accomplish still unfinished.

Haircut.

Shave.

Shower.

Plus, despite what Steve has told Felicity, I still have not actually made reservations for tonight and groan, knowing that finding something at this hour is going to be damn near impossible, despite who I am.

Calling in a favor would be a shitty thing to do at this stage in the game, even for a girl like Felicity.

I plop into my desk chair, giving myself just a few minutes of reprieve, shooting my stylist a note to let him know I'm running late.

He's cool with it, and I let out a sigh.

Firing up my computer, I type 'Last minute date options for the holiday,' into the search bar, hitting ENTER.

Lists pop up and I click on the first link — an itemized catalogue of dating ideas beginning with 'ordering carry-out and having a candlelight indoor picnic."

Nope, too intimate.

Find a local holiday lights display.

Nope, too cold.

Dancing? That could work, but I haven't been to a nightclub in ages — what if I find one and it sucks?

Ice skating in the park. Meh.

Wreath making? Gag.

Carriage ride, caroling, go to the bookstore and pick out a book for each other? What the fuck.

I'm screwed.

"I heard you were skulking around." A raspy voice scares the shit out of me from the doorway, and I jump in my chair, twisting my body to see none other than Shelia, with her gray hair and beady eyes judging me.

"Hey. Yeah, I wanted to pop in today one last time before the weekend."

"And you decided to wear that?"

My brow goes up. "Don't hold back, Sheila — tell me how you really feel."

"Aren't you still single?" she wants to know, powering ahead as if she hadn't just insulted my wardrobe. "You'll never find a classy woman dressed like the chimney sweep."

Jesus. "First of all, you know damn well I don't wear this shit every day. And secondly, barely anyone is here anymore."

Everyone has flown the coup. I probably need to check our company handbook because I could have sworn today was an official workday. Now I'm not so sure.

Her lips purse. "Nope, they're not. You kids and your work ethic these days ain't what it used to be. In my day, we'd never get away with half days and walking around eating bagels from a napkin."

Her loud voice and hawk-like pointed gaze trail Darren Powell as he scuttles by, terrified, bagel in one hand and a coffee in the other.

I roll my eyes. "Would you please stop scaring people?"

"That's no fun." She doesn't come in to take a seat, but she doesn't walk off, either. "There's not much else for me to do around here today, and if I head home, I'll be twiddling my thumbs until it's time to get ready for my date."

"Oh yeah?"

"Dwight's taking me to Sky Bar."

Sky Bar? What the hell, even I can't get into that place! I let out a low whistle, impressed. "Dang, Sheila — it's impossible to get a table there." I wonder if she'd be willing to sell me her reservation, and how much it would take to buy Dwight off.

"Dwight's nephew Kevin is the sous chef."

My brows lift again. Seriously, what the fuck?

"What about you?" She wants to know, always sticking her nose in my business. "What new ridiculously frou-frou place are you showing off tonight?"

Normally, I wouldn't tell her because the last thing I need are rumors swirling, started by the elderly receptionist, but in this case — what's the harm? Besides, I could use some advice considering I'm in a bind.

No reservations means no date.

Let's throw in the fact that I'm now living a lie, having to break the news to my date, who is going to react one of two ways:

1. Feel betrayed
2. Laugh it off and have fun the rest of the night.

I'll put money on the fact that Felicity will be light-hearted about it; from what I've seen so far, that woman is an upbeat, bundle of sexy cheerfulness.

Holiday cheer, most likely.

"Where you going tonight with your lady love?" Sheila wants to know, settling in at the door, waiting.

"Well see, that's the problem…" I begin. "I was so busy with getting through the holidays and making sure the reports were done around here, and athletes are getting hurt and agents are scrambling that I…"

I let my voice trail off and hope she can connect the dots on her own; fill in the blank, swoop in and fix my dilemma, because if Sheila is one thing — it's a fixer.

I wait.

Except, she doesn't speak.

"Hello?"

"This is a you problem," she huffs. "I'm tired of you men waiting until the last minute to plan shit because you haven't made your lady a priority."

"That's not what I was doing!" Okay, that's probably what I was doing — but it's not like I'd met Felicity before. How the hell was I supposed to know she was going to be this freaking amazing and gorgeous and perfect?

She's like the Christmas gift that keeps on giving.

"Sheila, please help me."

Sheila, the old bag, shakes her head no.

"I'm begging."

Her nose goes up. "That's not begging, that's telling me you're begging."

Good point. "What if I give you and Dwight tickets to every baseball game next season. Does he like baseball?"

She sniffs. "Eh."

"What does he even do?" I find myself asking.

"He owns a dry cleaner business, I'll have you know, and when people don't pick things up, he said he'd let me pick through the neglected items." The chin tilts higher. "We're talking *designer*." She emphasizes that last word haughtily.

"So does that mean he doesn't like baseball, or noo…"

"It means he can afford his own tickets." The receptionist pauses. "Unless it's a box suite."

Oh my god, this is extortion! "What about a week's paid vacation?"

Then again, I am attempting to bribe her.

"I take vacation *whenever* I want."

Accurate — she comes and goes as she pleases, knowing she isn't going to get fired, and I have a feeling money isn't a problem. There had to have been some kind of pension worked out with my grandfather before he passed. This woman could give two shits about the measly salary I pay her.

I inhale a deep breath. "Sheila, you've been with this company for over thirty years and you've seen me grow up here, and now you can see that my love life is a mess."

She nods.

"I share very little about my personal life, but I'll tell you this: I met someone incredible and if I don't pull a date out of my ass for tonight, the shit is going to hit the fan and she's going to hate me forever."

I leave out the part where I gave Felicity a fake name, pretended not to know her when we met, pretended to be a janitor, and told her there is a date at the end of this road we're on.

A good one.

A romantic one to ring in the new year.

She won't be kissing me when the ball drops if Sheila doesn't help me fix this, that's for damn sure—she'll be slapping my face.

Not that she seems like the violent type.

"You know what would be neat," Sheila finally says. "Have you ever seen that movie where the little kid plays matchmaker for his dad?"

I stare, clueless.

"The kid calls into a radio show about his dad being single and how he wants him to meet someone?"

The receptionist is glaring at me now, disgusted that I haven't any idea what movie she's talking about. "Anyway, the kid ends up writing this letter to this woman named Annie and tells him to meet the dad at the top of the Empire State Building on Valentine's Day." She pauses. "Or something like that, I don't know, it's been years."

"So… you want me to meet my date at the top of the Empire State Building several states away?" My eyes practically bug out of my skull. Is Sheila insane?

"No, you chump — the top of *this* building." She smiles, hit with a memory. "I once had a date set up a picnic lunch up top, but that was the 90s when men made more effort to woo a gal. Granted, he really only wanted to get in my pants, but it was a night I'll never forget. Like Rose on the Titanic."

Jesus, I didn't need to be reminded that Sheila is probably still out there sleeping with men, nor did I need to know our rooftop patio was defiled back when I was playing hide-and-seek up there with some of the board members' kids. If I didn't need a shower before, I feel the need to scrub more than once. Who knows what these hands have touched up there.

"You do know Jack would have fit on that raft." I can't help pointing out the obvious, much to her chagrin. "He didn't have to die."

She is not amused. "Do you want my help or not?"

"Yes."

"Then pick up that phone and call Timmy Wells. He's Skeeter's back up when that old bastard forgets to show up for work, and I'm pretty sure I saw him on the tenth floor earlier when I went down for a donut."

"Do you ever sit at your actual desk?"

"Rarely." She shoots a look at my phone.

"What am I supposed to say to him when he answers?"

"Tell him you need a favor, and that you'll pay him cash to stay tonight and open the roof, put a table and two chairs outside, drag some of the potted plants from the lobby on fifteenth, and the potted tree from eleven. Bonus if he can locate a few strings of lights, and a few heaters."

My mouth falls open. Christ, it's like she's done this before.

"Anything else?"

"That should do the trick." I don't move fast enough, and she's twirling her hand impatiently in the air to move me along. "And we're dialing… and we're dialing…"

Wow. She's worse than a honey badger, and twice as petrifying. I wonder what would happen if I didn't follow directions.

I pull up Timmy Wells number in the directory and call him rather than texting — he picks up immediately.

"Yeah?"

"Hi, um — Timmy." Why does it feel so odd calling a grown man Timmy? "This is Harrison McGinnis, up on the twenty-eight floor—"

"My *boss*, Harrison McGinnis?" He interrupts.

"Sure." I agree uncomfortably. "Listen Tim… my. I have a favor I need to ask of you and I hope you can accommodate me."

Sheila gives me an encouraging thumbs up.

"I seriously hate asking this of you, especially on your night off, but I'm willing to pay you for your time and effort."

The line is silent. Then, "I'm listening."

"I need someone who can get me onto the roof tonight for a date I'm trying to impress. And I need some things to accomplish that, and a reliable man to help me."

* * *

Me: *T-minus five hours until midnight.*

Felicity: *Does that also mean t-minus five hours until Date Time?*

Me: *If my math is correct it's only four and a half…*

Felicity: *Hey, I'm the number cruncher here…*

Me: *Okay okay okay — speaking of which, how was the rest of your day? You done yet?*

Felicity: *YES!!! **twirls and twirls in desk chair** DONE done done with my reports and can finally unchain myself from this desk! I'm about to shut everything down and blow this hot dog stand.*

Me: *That's great news! So it was a good day?*

I roll my eyes because I already know the answer to this, and by asking, I'm continuing to perpetuate the lie. But I'm also pimping her for information about myself, wondering if she'll spill the dirt on Harry — considering there were definitely sparks flying in both directions.

Oh, she hid it well, but they were there.

Me: *I lucked out today, I had a maintenance guy help me with a few things.*

At the mention of me, I perk up.

Me: *Oh yeah? What all did he do??*

Way too many question marks, bro.

I delete and start a new message.

Me: *OR SHE — sorry. Help you with?*

Felicity: *Lol it was a man. And I had this horrible situation with the light above my desk and he didn't just save the day, he saved my entire year. Literally.*

Me: *LOL your entire year?!*

Felicity: *Yes! Because I would have been done weeks ago if that light hadn't been messing with my head. As soon as he came along and fixed it, I was cranking out the work. It put me in such a good mood.*

What she means is HARRY put her in such a good mood.

I scowl, reading between the lines, oddly jealous since I AM HARRY.

HARRY IS ME.

Me: *You said he helped with a few things. Like what else?*

Felicity: *Well.... he fixed a drawer in my desk, opened the heater vent in the ceiling, and a vending machine inside the womens' bathroom I'd been complaining about LOLOL.*

Me: *They have vending machines in the bathroom?*

Felicity: *That was my polite way of saying "Tampon Machine"*

Me: *OH! It sounds like he was looking for random things to fix so he could hang around...*

It takes her a few minutes to respond and I imagine she's

searching for the proper response.

Felicity: *I can't speak for him, but maybe he lingered a bit longer than he should have. He wasn't being weird or anything if you're worried.*

Weird is the least of my worries, because I know you had chemistry with the guy.

Aka: ME.

Me: *You're a beautiful woman, I'm sure he couldn't help himself.*

Felicity: *Hmm, maybe. I doubt it.*

Me: *So — switching gears, really quick so you can get moving and get home; I have a time and location for you. Ready?*

Felicity: *Give it to me.*

My balls tighten, mind automatically going to sex and boobs and her hair in the palm of my hand.

Me: *Do you know where the McGinnis Building is on Downer Avenue?*

Felicity: *Um... I know that building very well, why?*

So she's not ready to tell me that's where she works? Okay — I get it. Fair enough.

Me: *At eleven o'clock, there's going to be a man in the lobby, and he's going to take you to the roof...*

* * *

THE HOT WATER beats down on me when I crank the heat on my six-jet shower, ready for the rest of the evening — thanking God for Sheila (of all people) and throwing up a hallelujah that I have an actual plan for tonight.

Once I finally got Sheila to see the problem with setting up a sex swing on the roof in December, not to mention as a first date with a virtual stranger, things started rolling and our ideas snowballed into what will hopefully be the most romantic first meeting Felicity has ever experienced.

At this exact moment, Timmy is setting up a beautiful winter themed setting, complete with Felicity's choice of finger foods compliments of yet another random connection Sheila has, cloth napkins, and a centerpiece full of her favorite Winter Camellias in various shades of pink and red.

While I probably should have fessed up to Felicity from the beginning about who I am, the benefit of going undercover in her office are the mental notes about all her favorites I was able to make on the sly. Without her knowing I was doing recon of her personal space.

Her computer screensaver? Has the same flower on it that's on her cheesy mug — it's pretty damn obvious she loves the winter flower. It also helps that my mom used to make me work at my aunt's flower shop every summer through high school. I probably wouldn't have recognized them otherwise.

One quick call to my aunt and I cleared out all her Winter Camellia inventory, along with that of some of her local colleagues, but for the right price it didn't seem to be an inconvenience for them at all.

The more the better.

Sheila and I were in agreement on *that* at least.

Is the entire thing cheesy? Maybe.

Is it over-the-top? Possibly.

Is she going to love it?

Absolutely.

And, hopefully the view makes up for the lies I have to expose, me being me and not Steve, that is.

If everything works out according to plan, there won't be a better view than the direct line of sight we have for the first-time-ever in our city NYE ball to drop at midnight.

Quickly I jack off in the shower, hoping to relieve myself of some of the lingering tension in my body, and maybe to keep myself from sporting a hard-on if Felicity shows up in a strappy dress. I'm a sucker for a woman's shoulders, but popping wood is probably not the best first impression to make.

I've got some fessing up to do before trying to take things to the next level.

I may be as hormonal as the next guy, but I'm not completely classless.

Shutting off the water and wrapping myself in a fluffy towel (no reason to cut corners when it comes to bathroom comfort), I begin doing a thorough trim on my beard. Just as I bring the electric razor to my cheek, my phone dings and my heart lurches.

Please don't let Felicity be cancelling, please don't let Felicity be cancelling, please don't let Felicity be cancelling…

It would be my luck if she ditches Steve for Harry.

My shoulders sag with relief when I see that it's Adam messaging me, and not my date.

Adam: *Hey man. Wanted to update you. Manuel Gomez is out for the rest of the season. Rotator cuff is busted, but he should be clear to continue contract negotiations.*

Me: *Dodged that bullet.*

Adam: *Also, Meg wants to know if your date is figured out.*

Me: *Dude. Do you have to share that shit with her? I'm her boss. I'd prefer her not spreading office gossip.*

Adam: *I tell my woman everything. And you're barely her boss. I'm more of her boss than you are.*

I shake my head. I really need to get with HR on that fraternization policy. After I'm grandfathered in, of course. Ha ha.

Me: *And you're barely her man. Two weeks doesn't count. Now leave me alone. I'm getting ready for my date.*

Adam: *So that's a yes? The date is a go...?*

Me: *Yes, dickhead. It's a go. Romantic rooftop rendezvous and all that shit.*

Adam: *The rooftop? OUR rooftop? You know I found a ball gag up there once with Sheila's name etched into the leather strap.*

I make a gagging sound no one but me can hear because I have learned too much about Sheila's sex life today. I cannot unlearn the things I've heard.

Me: *Thank you for giving me the need to bleach my brain.*

Adam: *Just doing my part. Make sure to sanitize before getting a little New Year's tickle for your pickle.*

Me: *Okay. I'm done with this now. See you next year.*

I toss my phone down and only glance over at it again when it gives me an alert that Adam replied. It's just a laughing emoji so I refuse to respond again. It's a good thing we're friends or I would have fired his ass a long time ago for not reporting that ball gag.

Hell, I still might.

It would serve the bastard right for keeping juicy information like that to himself, and I wonder if cameras should be installed up top; sounds like I'm not the only one who's been using it for extra-curricular activities.

I stare at myself in the foggy mirror, watching the water drip down my face from my hair, and stand taller.

It won't do if I'm freaking out about Felicity's reaction — I have to be confident I know her well enough by now that she's not going to bail on me when she sees me.

What an uncomfortable working environment that would be, especially now that Sheila's involved, Adam's been gossiping, and Meg probably knows.

Just send out a Memo on Monday. Give everyone the scoop at once, why don't they.

Groaning, I wipe the stray hairs from my face, drying it. This is why I never should have let that old busybody, Sheila, in on my business. Now she's going to stake a claim in my relationship and have opinions and such.

On the other hand, she is coordinating the entire thing, and if it weren't for her, there wouldn't be a date to get ready for.

A first date I'm going to be late for if I don't hurry my ass up.

I wipe my face and head to my closet where I grab my best black suit and sharpest white button down. It's time to go all out. This is the woman of my dreams, and I refuse to let it all go down in a flaming pile of New Year's poo.

FELICITY

$\mathcal{I}$ am thoroughly showered and shampooed.

I am groomed in my nether regions.

In fact, I'm so groomed downtown, I had to break my self-imposed *No Shave All Winter Months* clause in the event I decide to ring-a-ling-ling in the new year with a little action — if you catch my drift.

And yet, I'm not all that excited to be here…

How horrible is that? A night I've been looking forward to for over a week — since the night Steve finally found the courage to ask to meet me.

Sighing as I wait for the elevator doors to open, I silently curse Harry for sucking the anticipation out of me like a pleasure vacuum, without even bothering to ask for my phone number.

Was I too forward with him? Was I not forward *enough*? I did my best when he was scuttling around my office, fixing things, to remain professional. Tried my best not to drop hints of my attraction, ending up with nothing to show for it except an unenthusiastic attitude for a meet up that should have been the most exciting night of my life!

146

Damn Skeeter for leaving me with the hottest man I've ever met and distracting me from tonight's goal: meeting the man of my dreams.

At least I look hot.

My reflection in the elevator doors may be slightly distorted, but there's no hiding my shape in the dress I chose for tonight. It may be long sleeve and high necked, but it's a short Bodycon dress that hugs me in all the right places.

And I do mean ALL of them.

Hmm. Actually…

I turn sideways and the image is distorted just enough to make my boobs even bigger and my waist smaller. Nice ass. Great legs.

Dang girl! Get it!

I am seriously contemplating snapping a pic of my bombshell reflection for social media, when the elevator dings making me jump. Forces me to walk through the door and step into the car that will take me to the rest of my life.

Wow. Meg was right. I am super theatrical.

Focus, Felicity.

Focus on Steve, Felicity. *Steve.*

Not Harry, who I wish I was here with, but Steve who I am now wishing will be a dud so I can go home, put on my jammies, and pull out my vibrator while Harry's beautiful face is still freshly vivid in my mind.

I press the button to the rooftop floor and say a quick Hail Mary that this elevator can make it all the way to the top. Which leads to the one thing that has been bothering me all night — why here? Of all the rooftops in the city, of all the buildings, why did Steve choose the place I work as the site of our first meet up and how the hell did he coordinate this?

Suddenly I feel my gut telling me something is off with him. I don't get stalker vibes, but I also can't put a finger on what the niggling feeling could be. I guess I'm about to find out, like it or not.

Or. I'm about to be murdered.

Could go either way.

I dig through my purse. *Dammit, where is my mace?*

The elevator dings once I'm all the way to the top — a place I've never been — and I admit to being surprised there were no lurches or lunges or groans on the way up.

I bet Harry already got someone in here to fix it, I can't help thinking. He's just so damn efficient.

And kind.

And hot.

And smells like man, and can do all the manly things, like fix stuff.

Shit. Steve is fifty feet away from me and I'm daydreaming about someone else! No wonder I was in dating Droughtlandia for so long. I'm a fucking mess!

The doors retract, revealing a brightly lit vestibule and an older man in uniform waiting to greet me. He's tall but hunched over, wrinkled face weathered with age.

I groan.

If Meg was right and I *have* been catfished, I'm going to be sooo pissed.

"Are you… Steve?" I question, trying to keep the venom out of my voice on the off chance I'm wrong.

The old man smirks, no doubt enjoying my confusion and finding the whole thing hilarious. That's a good sign, right?

We can laugh about it when I turn tail and leave.

"No ma'am. My name is Fritz, I work for your date. May I take your wrap and clutch for you?"

This man works for Steve? Like, is he a butler?

Wow. Steve pulled out all the stops if he's trying to impress me by bringing his staff all the way up here on a holiday.

"I think I might need it. It's cold out tonight." And the roof is going to be twenty times worse than it is on the ground thirty stories below.

"Rest assured, ma'am, there are plenty of heaters on the deck. It's nice and toasty out there if I do say so myself." He stands taller with pride.

"Oh." I glance down and realize the dress really does look stellar without the wrap. Even if I have a need for it later, first impressions win over, and I hand the kind gentleman my things. "Well in that case, thank you."

"Are you ready?" Fritz asks, and am I mistaken or are his eyes twinkling?

No. I'm not.

"Yes, thank you. Lead the way."

Fritz gives me his arm to take and I loop my hand through as he pulls open the door, my breath hitching as I take in the beauty of the sight before me.

Winter Camellias cover just about every square inch of the space, their fragrance stronger than I would have ever expected. The red, pink, and white flowers create a canopy from the outside world. Tiny white twinkly lights are weaved through the trellises, making everything seem to glow.

Twinkle. *Glow.*

A table for two sits in the middle of it all, boasting a gorgeous centerpiece with more of my favorite blooms floating amongst tea candles. The tablecloth is crisp and the place settings are sparkling.

Candles, candles everywhere.

Stunning.

And Fritz was right; I don't even see the heaters, probably hidden behind all the flowers, and while there's a nip in the air, the temperature is pleasant.

I won't freeze.

A bit begrudgingly, I have to admit — if this is the way Steve impresses a girl, I could have done worse. This set-up is impressive and amazing.

In the corner, a man is stepping out from the shadows.

A man I… recognize.

A man I've been thinking and daydreaming about; a man I thought about while riding the elevator to this very roof.

My eyes damn near bug out of my skull, lashes fluttering.

"Harry?"

My heart picks up speed as my brain runs through all the scenarios. Did *he* help set this up? Does he know Steve? Did my date hire him to serve dinner because Harry works in the building? Is Harry a catfish? Is Steve?

This cannot be happening. Am I caught on the damn roof with a man I'm here to meet and the man I've been lusting after for the past several hours?

Questions play on a loop in my mind, stomach in knots.

I want to barf, but Fritz took my bag, and I refuse to ruin these shoes.

"Hi Felicity."

The more I look at him, the more I realize he's not dressed like part of the serving staff. In fact, he's not dressed like a maintenance man at all.

I take a few steps forward. "What are you doing here?"

He smooths his hand down his tie and I swear he takes a long, steadying breath before saying, "We have a date."

My eyes look back and forth at his, trying to make heads or tails of the situation.

"No. I have a date with Steve. You are not him."

He takes a step forward stopping right in front of me and a gust of wind blows; he smells so good. Better than he had earlier in the day, and even in my three-inch heels I have to look up at him.

He is that tall and commanding.

Swoon.

"Felicity, I'm… Steve."

Naturally, my head gives a little shake. "No. You're Harry."

"Right."

So is he agreeing with me, after he just told me his name is Steve?

"So what, like you have two names?"

"Yes. Like almost everyone. My full name is Harrison…"

Harry…

"Steven…"

Steve…

"McGinnis."

McGin…

"Wait… WHAT??" I'm practically shouting now. "You're…"

My brain works overtime, connecting the dots: He was on my floor today because he was working. He had keys to all the offices and closets because it is his company. He set up our date on top of the building because HE OWNS IT.

Pointing at him I accuse, "You're Harrison McGinnis. Mr. McGinnis. My *boss*."

He bobbles his head from side to side. "Technically, Victoria is your boss. I'm just her boss."

Oh, he's going to be cute about it now?

"That is not helping." I pace the small area, trying not to hyperventilate, all the excitement and anticipation I had, fizzling like the champagne in the glasses nearby. "You… you're… Why did you tell me your name was Harry?"

He shrugs like this is no big deal. Au contraire, Mister. This is a huge deal. "My name *is* Harry. Just… Harrison."

"But I had you fixing my light and my heater and… oh my god you fixed the tampon machine!"

That's it. I have to find another job. Forget seniority. Forget my extra comp day. I'm officially humiliated and need to pack my things and move across the country immediately.

"I fixed the tampon machine because it needed to be fixed. And I… are you okay Felicity?"

I'm fanning myself, breathing heavily. Why can't I catch a breath?

"Is it hot out here?"

"No, it's actually on the chilly side." His eyes flash concern and he's immediately at my side. "Come sit down." Guiding me into the world's most comfortable dining chair because of the extra fluffy cushion on the seat, he hands me a glass of water. "Drink this."

I do as he instructs, the cool liquid confirming how very hot the rest of me is as it slides down my throat. Closing my eyes, I take a few deep, calming breaths, concentrating on how good Harry smells. And oh man does he. I could eat him up. After I eat up this dinner of course because did I see empanadas?

Finally feeling like I have myself under control again, I slowly open my eyes to see Harry staring at me, concern written all over his face.

"Better?" he asks gently, taking the glass from my hand and placing it on the table.

"Much, thank you." I look around the rooftop again and notice all the little details that have gone into tonight — thousands of my favorite flowers, a carafe of chocolate milk on the table, a direct view to the brand new New Year's Eve ball from my seat. Harry, Harrison… Mr. McGinnis, put in so much effort just for me. "I don't understand what's happening."

He nods once and stands, making his way to the opposite chair. "It's kind of a long story. Shall we eat while I tell it?" He gestures to his seat and I nod my approval.

As he tucks his legs under the table, a man I assume is a waiter comes out and begins pouring champagne into sparkling clear flutes. He then proceeds to fill our plates with a variety of appetizers and small finger foods — enough to give us a good taste of everything while filling me up in the process.

Once we're alone again, I pick up a mini quiche and blow on it before addressing Harry directly. "Who are you really?"

He pops what I have since learned is a meat and cheese empanada in his mouth and chews, wiping his lips with a napkin before answering. "Like I said, I'm Harrison Steven McGinnis. Most people call me Harrison. You've already figured out I'm the guy in charge of this company, but like you found out today, I also like to get my hands dirty sometimes."

"Yeah, explain that. I don't know many CEO's who go around fixing squeaky drawers on the last day of the year. Come to think of it, your knowledge of acquisitions makes more sense now."

"And for the record, I'm impressed with your knowledge of them as well." He chuckles deep in his chest and now that I know Harry is Steve and Steve is Harry, I have zero guilt about enjoying that sound. He takes a sip of his champagne and continues. "I like tinkering. If something's broken, I usually know how to fix it. And with Skeeter on vacation. and me having some free time, it doesn't hurt to pitch in."

"Skeeter is off. That makes so much more sense now."

"That nothing was getting done?" I nod. "You could have just had the office manager call him about it."

I narrow my eyes, getting real irritated by people trying to force that middle man on me.

"Or not," he tacks on with a playful smile.

Trying and failing at attempting the dainty way of cutting meat off a chicken wing, I give up and rip it right off the bone with my fingers.

"But when you figured out who I was, because it's obvious you did," I gesture at the milk in front of us as evidence, "why didn't you tell me?"

He runs his hand through his thick hair which I just realized has been cleaned up around his neckline. Wow. He really did pull out all the stops for me.

"It threw me off guard at first. Here was this super cute employee spouting off directions on regular maintenance and demanding I not leave until it was done. It was funny."

I groan. "Now that I know who you are, that's not funny. I could have been fired."

"Yeah, because it's such a smart idea to fire the only person in accounting who bothers to come in on the last day of the year."

"Touché. And yet, you didn't call me out."

He shakes his head and sips the champagne again. "Steve, that's my online alter ego in case you haven't figured that out yet…"

"We'll get to him later."

"Noted. Steve isn't all that great at planning romantic dates. He had a few ideas and was close to nailing one down, but when he met you, he decided it was best to get some insider information about the lucky woman he got to go on a date with tonight."

I snort a laugh. "And let me guess, then Sheila showed up and helped you plan the perfect rooftop romance."

Harry, er… Harrison's jaw drops open and he stares at me in shock. "How'd you know she helped?"

"Pretty sure the waiter is her sister's nephew Andrew. She hired him to carry hors d'oeuvres around at the Christmas party a couple weeks ago."

"Dammit Sheila. She swore she was going to be stealthy on her involvement."

"Have you met Sheila? She is absolutely going to take credit for helping with this. Oh and be warned, the second she figures out I'm the one you did all this for, she's going to call you New Year's Steve from now on."

"New Year's… what?"

"Inside joke. I'm letting you in on it so just roll with it."

"I will never understand that woman."

"Probably best that you don't. What I don't understand, though, is why Steve? Why all the secrecy and going by your middle name on LoveSwept?"

"That's the part I feel the worst about. I didn't like hiding myself from you. Especially the more we got to know each other."

"So why did you?"

He sucks in a breath and blows it out. "I've had some bad experiences with women."

"Describe bad experiences."

"They could have been much worse, I admit that. But it's never fun when you realize a woman is dating you for your money. Or for your business. Or for the status your money and business will bring her. It's not like the name Harrison McGinnis is all that common. One Google search and…"

"… and the sharks circle in the underground parking lot."

"Exactly. I'm not about that. Yes, I have more money than most people in this town. Yes, as our agents sign more and more quality clientele, the company gets bigger. And yes, I'm the man in charge of all that. But at the end of the day, I'm also the guy who is going to grab the ten-foot ladder and change the light-bulbs in his ceiling and is going to do a DIY if he feels like it and hates scary movies because his nightmares are vivid."

"That was oddly specific."

"If you're going to see the real me, I might as well tell you the truth and that is, I am a wienie. I also jog in case I need the endurance someday during the zombie apocalypse because I don't have to be the fastest runner. I just have to be faster than the last person. If that's you, I've enjoyed our time together."

He says it so nonchalantly I can't help but laugh, especially when the shit eating grin crosses his face.

"You're a hot mess, you know that?"

"I do. And that's the guy you've been getting to know. Harry, or Steve, who just slaps on deodorant to pop in the office after a run. Not Harrison McGinnis, the CEO and majority shareholder of the McGinnis Agency."

"Is that why you looked like you work in maintenance today? You didn't shower before coming in?" I'm not sure why that thought makes me happy, but it does. Maybe because it reiterates how down to earth he really is.

"I hope I didn't smell too bad."

There is pleading in his piercing blue eyes. A longing for me to accept him for who he is, not what he comes with. I have to admit, his insecurity in this moment is hella sexy.

I shake my head and bat my eyelashes just a bit. "Not too bad at all. In fact, I may have gotten a whiff or two that made me want to jump you."

He belts out a belly laugh and my heart skips a beat. All day I've been thinking about Harry and feeling guilt about Steve when they've been the same person all along. And I get why he did it. He wants someone who is genuinely interested in him. Considering I was ready to jingle his balls when he was an hourly worker, I think I'm a safe bet.

He rests his forearms on the table and leans in. "Am I forgiven for the lies by omission?"

"There's nothing to forgive. I understand completely. And I'm glad you made sure this was a real connection before throwing your money around. If there weren't extenuating circumstances, all this," I wave my hand at the extravagant set up, "could be kind of intimidating."

"But not to you, right?"

"Knowing Sheila is involved, I'd say this is actually pretty toned down."

The noise on the street below increases in volume and I can only imagine it's almost that time.

Harrison stands and holds out his hand to me. "Come on. Let's get ready to ring in the New Year."

I take his hand and thread my fingers through his, following where he leads me. Closer to the ledge and away from the heaters, I begin to shiver. Harrison immediately moves behind me and wraps arms around my shoulders, enveloping me in his warmth. His body feels just like I knew it would — hard in all the right places with a softness to his touch.

"Is this okay?" he whispers in my ear and I shiver again,

although this time it's not from the cold. Oh no. This one is all lady bits.

"It's perfect."

We watch as the giant ball several blocks away illuminates, the lights below it dancing as if they're getting ready for the count-down with us. In a matter of seconds, it begins to lower, changing colors every second as we count down.

Ten... nine... eight...

I turn my head and look up at Harrison who isn't paying any attention to the scene in front of us, instead staring down at me with a lust-filled gaze.

Seven... six... five...

When he realizes I'm looking back at him, he turns me in his arms so we're standing face to face.

Four... three... two...

As the clock counts down and the ball drops, Harrison takes my face in his hands and leans in, so close I can almost taste him.

One...

His lips drop to mine as the crowds in the street erupt into cheers and well-wishes. I hear none of it, so focused on this kiss. *This kiss.* A kiss full of promise and hope and a mutual future, with just enough passion to make it exciting and just enough reserve to have me wanting more. It's the best kind of kiss to ring in the new year with my New Year's Steve.

Er... *New Year's Harrison.*

That has a nice ring to it, don't ya think?

ACKNOWLEDGMENTS

And now... our version of Auld Lang Syne...

M.E. Carter: *Should auuuuuuuld acquaintance beeeeeeee forgot... and neeeeeever brought to miiiiiiind?*

Sara NEY: *Why are you singing? You always do this.*

M.E. Carter: *I'm feeling nostalgic. Do you realize how long it's been since we've written a book together? Since the last time — 2015 I think?? We've both moved and collectively dropped 400 pounds of man between our divorces...*

Sara: *But two of our kids have both turned into pre-teens so really, who is the winner here?*

M.E.: *Hmm. Good point.*

Sara: *On the other hand, we've both been decorating for the holidays in like, October...*

M.E.: *Speak for yourself, I put my Christmas tree up in late November.*

Sara: *Covid made me do it early.*

M.E.: *Do IT? We are still talking about Christmas trees, aren't we?*

Sara: *Unfortunately... yes.*

M.E.: *Bwahahahah.* Well, the good news is, we managed to share a little more romance with the world. What are you doing for New Year's this year?

Sara: *Uh. The same thing I do every year; eat shrimp, watch tv, and fall asleep around 10:00... What about you???*

M.E.: *Apparently, I'm coming to your house because you have shrimp. And less children.*

Sara: *Before you and your facemask hop on that plane, we probably* *need to thank a couple people for putting up with us and these crazy ideas.*

M.E.: *Nothing says "holiday cheer" like a surprise book for everyone to squeeze in.*

Sara: *And squeeze we do. First up is Letitia Hassar for designing this adorable cover! Harrison ended up with a beard because of it.*

M.E.: *I mean, it's a reasonable assumption he would have ended up with one anyway. RAWR.*

Sara: *Listen, I know it's been a while but calm your hormones lady.*

M.E.: *Sorry, sorry. We also need to thank Jennifer Van Wyk who didn't just edit for us last minute, she also waited for us to give it to her because deadline? What's that?*

Sara: *Yeeeeaah. I'm just going to avoid eye contact for a while.*

M.E.: *Probably a good idea.*

Jennifer: ****pops head in**** *Did someone say shrimp? I feel like I deserve some because of my comments alone. GOLD, I tell you. Pure. Gold. Also, I accept tips like "Harry" was going to give accounting. Spa day? Pizza?*

M.E.: *Man, editors are getting demanding these days, aren't they? Anywho...we also need to thank Shauna for formatting and PR and all things organization. Well done!!*

Sara: *And then of course the fabulous reader groups we couldn't do this without. Ney's Little Lattes and Carter's Cheerleaders. And that's not even the tip of the iceberg! There are so many great places to find fellow readers.*

M.E.: *There really are. But you know the best place to find budding readers? With our kiddos, who we do everything for because they're the best, aren't they?*

Sara: *100% agree. So we leave you with these parting words: thank you. From the bottom of our hearts.*

M.E.: *You are truly appreciated. And now, it's time to sing again.*

Sara: *No it's really not.*

M.E.: *Yes it is. Come to the microphone with me Sara and unleash* *your inner girl band. Should aaauuud acquaintance beeeee forgot and daaaaaays of aud lang syne!*

Sara: *We're outta here...*

Did you enjoy our writing style? We certainly enjoyed writing it for you! But wait! There's more! If you haven't read FriendTrip yet, it's available now and free for Kindle Unlimited subscribers! (add links here) Here's a sneak peek:

SNEAK PEAK OF FRIENDTRIP

*B*ecky
The Early Years

"When I get married, it's forever." This announcement comes from my best friend Janine. "Seriously, you guys—one and done. Divorce will not be an option."

I roll my eyes and pull back the top on the white pizza box, wielding the sharp metal cutter. "Famous last words."

Call me cynical, but her declaration makes me cringe every time she makes it. And she's been making it a lot lately. Janine is crazy if she thinks her relationship is going to be perfect. No one's is. Take my parents for example: both of them married and divorced no less than five times between them, and each of them proclaiming "this is the one" with every trip down the aisle. Or beach. Or Vegas chapel. Or courthouse.

"I'm just saying, Becky," Janine continues, talking and chewing at the same time. She always does this and it drives me freaking nuts. So gross. "When I get married, it *will* be for forever. No divorce. People don't make enough effort to keep their marriages together. They just bail at the first hint of trouble. I know couples who've been married three or four times!"

She clamps her mouth shut so fast I can actually hear her teeth knock together, and shoots me an apologetic expression. It's clear she just remembered my parents' multiple marriages.

"The system makes it too easy to get divorced," I intone, letting her off the hook. I slide two huge slices of pepperoni pizza onto my paper plate. Maggiano's is *the* best pizza in town, possibly on this side of the Mississippi, and watch as a long, gooey trail of cheese hangs onto the slice by a thread when I lift it to my watering mouth.

I close my eyes and groan out loud.

It's cheesy.

It's greasy.

It's thin crust.

It's pizza night.

Pizza night… the sole night of the week we're free to stay in, order out, and spend some quality time with each other—preferably in our pajamas, sans make-up, no men allowed.

As juniors in college, we have *very* demanding academic schedules and a catalog rotation of nightly socials. Janine and I came up with the general breakdown our freshman year to stay organized and never deviate.

Wednesday: The Escape Club for dancing. The EC has the greatest DJs, the best dancing, and some of the best jams from the seventies. Janine considers Wednesday night her time to shine, and her one night of weekly cardio. Basically, whooping it up until she sweats is the only exercising she's willing to do. You haven't lived until you've heard my bestie belt out "Summer Nights" with John Travolta and Olivia Newton-John. Janine loves *Grease*. We still have it on VHS (even though the DVD would be clearer and our VCR is on its last leg and makes a horrific noise when we start it up or rewind the tape) and have seen it no less than a hundred times. She is a *stickler* for authenticity. She never fails to get pissed when a drunken co-ed sings a verse wrong, or out of tune.

Thursday: Midnight Rodeo night. Another night of dancing, but the two-stepping variety, which involves more muscle and less cardio. While it's not my favorite, we get to leave our bootcut jeans at home. Janine thoroughly enjoys the view of a cowboy in tight jeans. Midnight Rodeo night is the perfect excuse to break out my cowboy boots, cowgirl hat, and Daisy Dukes, because let's face it, we won't have these size two asses forever.

Friday: On- or off-campus parties. Where there's a house party, there's Becky and Janine. Just last week, Janine won a quarters tournament at an on-campus dorm party, and the prize was two pub-crawl tee shirts. Score!

Saturday: Greek night. Specifically reserved for whatever fraternity or sorority party is going on. Janine loves any excuse to tie on a toga. Last weekend, her mission was to get me drunk on "trashcan punch". She succeeded, and we left the frat house with Greek letters written in Sharpie pen across our boobs. Fortunately, we sobered up before we made it to the tattoo parlor and permanently etched the letters into our skin. It seemed like a good idea at the time because that night was *awesome*.

Sunday: Good Samaritan Day. If you count helping our fraternity friends finish off their kegs before they're needed back at the liquor store as being Good Samaritans, then we're guilty as charged! No one wants them to lose their deposits if the kegs are late, so really, we're helping to promote fiscal responsibility.

Monday: Recuperation Night. Sleep. All. Day. Well, obviously not if we have class, but I'm not sure either of us stay awake past eight o'clock on Monday nights. Not after five straight days of partying...

See? Demanding. Exhausting. *Sigh...* the life of a college student.

Which leaves us tonight: Tuesday pizza night with the girls.

I filter Janine's voice over the sound of my own chewing and tune in to hear her say,

"I mean, if I'm going to marry the love of my life, I owe it to him to see past his mistakes and try to work it out."

She gives her dark brown hair a flip, and her giant hoop earrings sway.

I crinkle my nose as I look at her in disbelief. "What. Ever. If my husband ever steps out on me, his ass is mine. It's like TLC says, don't go chasing waterfalls. If he wants to stray, he needs to go."

Our friend Jennifer Stiltner grimaces. "Okay, first of all, I don't even understand that analogy because I don't listen to your music from a decade ago. Secondly, no man is ever going to cheat on us."

Janine nods her agreement. "And how do you plan on making sure *that* never happens? You're not Mariah Carey. You can't just make men bend to your will."

"The plan is easy," I say, licking the grease dripping down my thumb. "I'm going to make it a point to stay a sex kitten in the bedroom. A man won't stray if his needs are being met."

Janine points to me dramatically. "That, my friend, is a solid plan. We should all do that."

Both my friends nod in agreement because I'm truly a genius.

AH, but the best made plans don't usually come to fruition do they? Meet Becky and Janine in FriendTrip, available now. Just scan the QR code to grab a copy!

SCAN ME